Chronicles of the Grim Reaper
Volume 1

A journey through the eyes of the one who sees all endings but is never part of the story—until now.

GRIZ CALDERON

CALLIOPEZEN
PUBLISHING LLC

Chronicles of the Grim Reaper
Volume I
by Griz Calderon

Copyright © 2025 by Griz Calderon
All rights reserved

No part of this book may be reproduced or transmitted in any form or by any means, electronic or mechanical, including photocopying, recording, or by any information storage and retrieval system, without permission in writing from the publisher, except for brief quotations used in reviews.

Edited by Colm Farren
Cover Design by George Long

Published by Calliopezen Publishing LLC
Richardson, TX

Trade Paperback ISBN: 979-8-9919729-8-7
Hardcover ISBN: 979-8-9919729-6-3
Digital ISBN: 979-8-9919729-7-0
Audio ISBN: 979-8-9919729-9-4
First Edition: April 22, 2025
Printed in U.S.A.

Website: https://chroniclesofthegrimreaper.com/
YouTube: https://www.youtube.com/@ChroniclesoftheGrimReaper

The characters and events in this book are fictional. Any resemblance to real persons, living or dead, is purely coincidental.

To my love, my sisters, and my parents,
for inspiring me to dream,
for encouraging me to write,
and for always being there with love and support.

This book is for you.

Preface

When I began writing *Chronicles of the Grim Reaper*, my goal was simple: to tell stories that would resonate with readers on a deeply human level. Death is a universal experience, yet how we approach it—through fear, curiosity, or reverence—varies widely. I wanted to explore this spectrum by reimagining the Grim Reaper, not as a figure to fear, but as a compassionate presence offering solace, guidance, and understanding in life's most defining moments.

These stories touch on universal themes: love, loss, redemption, justice, and hope. They explore the emotional intricacies of the human experience, connecting life's fragility with its resilience. My hope is that this collection encourages readers to reflect on their own journeys, offering moments of comfort, thoughtfulness, and even inspiration.

Chronicles of the Grim Reaper is not just a series of tales about endings but also about beginnings.

From the very first story, my intention was to invite readers into the Reaper's world and challenge traditional perceptions. These tales reveal him as more than a harbinger of death. He is a steady presence in moments of transition, offering guidance and reflection in the most pivotal moments of a soul's journey.

As the collection grew, I uncovered additional dimensions to the Reaper's existence. Some stories focus on peace and acceptance, while others explore the challenges and complexities of passing. Each tale highlights something unexpected: a significant bond, an act of justice, or a lasting insight into the nature of life and death.

Together, these stories form a collection of meaningful encounters, offering insight into not only the Reaper's role but also the lives he touches. Whether comforting, bittersweet, or reflective, each story contributes to a broader narrative that reimagines what it means to face the inevitable.

As you immerse yourself in this collection, may these stories leave you captivated and moved, inspiring reflection on the themes they present: the resilience of the human spirit, the bonds we share, and the beauty found in the transitions that shape us.

Contents

The Doorway to Forever   1

1. The Ending   2
2. The Beginning   6

Echoes of the Past   10

3. The First Harvest   11
4. The Quilt   16
5. The Gift   22

Shadows of Understanding   25

6. The Presence in the Shadows   26
7. The Visit   30

Ripples of Justice   35

8. Between Worlds   36
9. The Price of Deception   41
10. The Timekeeper   44
11. The Hunt   48

Marks of the Unseen   54

12.	The Witnesses	55
13.	The Last Witness	60

Fading Light — 66

14.	The Day the Sky Fell	67
15.	The Last Breath	70

Unyielding Spirits — 72

16.	The Fight Against the Darkness	73
17.	The Reunion	77
18.	The Choice	83
19.	A Quiet Sacrifice	90

End of an Age — 94

20.	Wings of Valor	95

Voices of the Wild — 100

21.	Keeper of Hearts	101
22.	Into the Abyss	106
23.	Eternal Waters	109

Paths Unwritten — 112

24.	The Bridge	113
25.	Fates Passing	116

Whisper Between Worlds — 119

26.	The Silent Plea	120
27.	The Silent Embrace	124
28.	The Dance	127

29. The Final Farewell	130
The Fragile Horizon	134
30. Light in the Darkness	135
31. The Light of Day	139
32. An Inexplicable Calm	143
33. The Fractured Mind	146
Paths to Redemption	157
34. Signs	158
35. A Light Returns	162
Ashes of Renewal	167
36. The Forest	168
37. The Fallen	172

Every end is a new beginning.

The Doorway to Forever

Every ending holds the promise of a new beginning toward something unexpected and meaningful.

The Ending

JACOB LAY ON THE stretcher in the back of the speeding ambulance, the paramedics working frantically around him. The harsh, rhythmic beeping of machines filled the small space, blending with the blaring siren that resonated through the mountains. The setting sun cast shadows across the rocky landscape, the sky painted in shades of orange and pink, evoking a serenity in stark contrast to the urgency inside the ambulance.

His pulse was weak, barely there, and his body was battered from the impact of the accident. Yet, his soul lingered, caught between this world and the next. He could see the paramedics working on him, their hands moving quickly, their voices muffled as if he were underwater. But Jacob wasn't focused on them. His gaze kept drifting to the mountains outside, the same mountains he had navigated countless times.

Just a few hours earlier, Jacob had been riding down a quiet highway near Pocatello, Idaho, wearing his favorite yellow cycling top. The color had always made him feel vibrant, alive—perfect for a day like today. He was on his way to his cousin's wedding, planning to squeeze in a long ride before the ceremony. Weddings were always a bit awkward for Jacob, and this one would be especially so since he'd be attending alone, but the ride had been his way of clearing his mind.

He recalled the moment he had noticed the yellow Jeep in his rearview mirror, its driver a woman with long auburn hair. Something about that Jeep had caught his attention, though he couldn't pinpoint why. He remembered thinking how the bright yellow of her vehicle matched his cycling top. It was just a passing thought, quickly overshadowed by the sheer joy of the ride and the anticipation of pushing his limits.

Jacob had always been a man driven by adventure. The outdoors were his sanctuary, a place where he could escape from the expectations of others and live life on his terms. He had climbed mountains, kayaked in remote lakes, and even jumped out of planes—all in search of that next thrill. Relationships had never lasted long; his passion for adventure was too consuming, and the women he dated eventually drifted away, unable to compete with his need to explore the world.

He remembered the time he cycled through the rolling hills of Tuscany, the vineyards stretching out in every direction, the sun warm on his back. He could still taste the wine from the small village he had stopped in, the rich, earthy flavor mingling with the sense of accomplishment from the day's ride.

He thought about the time he had hiked through the dense forests of the Pacific Northwest, the air thick with the scent of pine and earth. The stillness of the forest had been an antidote to the chaotic energy of the city, a reminder of the peace he found in solitude. These moments had defined his life, giving him a sense of purpose and fulfillment that nothing else could.

Jacob felt a pang of regret. Not for the life he had lived—he had no regrets about that—but for the life he hadn't had the chance to live. He had always imagined that one day, he would find someone who shared his love for adventure, someone who could keep up with him. But now, it seemed that day would never come.

His thoughts returned to the moment of the accident. He had seen the car in his mirror, the one that had swerved to avoid an oncoming truck. It all happened so fast. The vehicle had missed the truck but veered directly into his path. He had no time to react; the impact was sudden and brutal. He remembered the sensation of being thrown from his bike, the world spinning around him before everything went dark.

Jacob glanced at the paramedics again, seeing their faces etched with concentration and concern. They were doing everything they could to save him, but Jacob knew, deep down, that it wasn't enough. His body was too broken, too damaged. He could feel his grip on life slipping away, like sand slipping through his fingers.

The mountains outside the ambulance window seemed to glow with the last light of the day, and Jacob found himself entranced by the sight. He felt a strange acceptance, a quiet understanding that his time was coming to an end. The sun was setting on his life, just as it was setting on the day.

As his vision began to blur, Jacob became aware of a presence beside him. He hadn't noticed anyone else in the ambulance, but now, there was someone there, standing silently, watching him. He turned his head slightly and saw a figure in a deep, dark robe, with a hood that obscured most of his face. The Grim Reaper.

Jacob wasn't afraid. In fact, he felt a sense of calm as the Reaper stepped closer. The figure's face was mostly hidden, but Jacob could sense the Reaper's gaze on him, steady and understanding.

"You've lived a good life, Jacob," the Reaper said, his voice low and soothing, like a distant echo. "You've seen the world, experienced things most people only dream of. But now, your journey here is coming to an end."

Jacob nodded weakly, his mind swirling with memories and thoughts of what could have been. He wanted to say something, to ask questions, but he found that he couldn't speak. The words were stuck in his throat, lost in the haze of his fading consciousness.

The Reaper seemed to understand. He reached out, placing a skeletal hand on Jacob's shoulder, a gesture of comfort rather than threat. "Don't worry," the Reaper continued. "Your journey isn't over. It's just beginning. There's more waiting for you, more than you could ever imagine."

As the Reaper spoke, the sounds of the ambulance began to fade, the beeping of the machines growing distant, the voices of the paramedics fading into silence. The mountains outside the window blurred into a soft glow, and Jacob felt himself being pulled away from the world he had known.

The Reaper shook his head slowly. "No, Jacob. This is not the end. It's just the beginning. Your journey has only just begun."

And with that, the Reaper gently took Jacob's soul, leading him away from the ambulance, away from the scene of his accident. As they walked, the world around them began to fade, the mountains, the trees, the setting sun—all of it dissolving into a soft, comforting light. Jacob felt at peace, ready for whatever came next. He didn't know where the Reaper was taking him, but he wasn't afraid.

The Beginning

MADDIE STOOD IN FRONT of the large mirror in her bedroom, just as she had when she was a little girl. The mirror had seen countless versions of her over the years—dressed in sparkly shoes and princess gowns, imagining herself as a fairytale princess like the ones in the bedtime stories her father used to read to her, his voice bringing each character to life. Those were moments she cherished, moments that shaped who she was.

As Maddie grew older, her love for dresses didn't fade, though they became less about fairytales and more about real life events. Weddings, to be specific. She had a closet full of bridesmaid dresses, each one a token of a friend she had stood beside on their special day.

But despite all the weddings she had attended, she had never been the bride. She had come close a few times, but something always went wrong. Her relationships never lasted, and she often found herself wondering why. Why wasn't she good enough? Why did her partner's always seem to find someone else right after breaking up with her?

Maddie tried not to dwell on it, but it was hard not to feel the sting of loneliness. She wanted what everyone else seemed to have—someone to share her life with, someone who loved her for who she was. But that dream always seemed just out of reach. Still, she put on a brave face, smiling through the sadness, always the supportive friend, even when her heart was breaking.

Today was no different. She was on her way to yet another wedding, dressed in a pretty pink dress with strappy silver heels. The drive to Pocatello, Idaho, was a familiar one, the winding roads taking her through the beautiful mountain scenery she loved so much. The wind blew through her long auburn hair as she drove her yellow Jeep, the fresh mountain air filling her lungs. She had always loved the mountains, the way they seemed to stretch on forever, offering a sense of freedom she couldn't find anywhere else.

As she drove, Maddie's thoughts drifted, as they often did, to her own life. She thought about the friends who had found love, the weddings she had attended, and the relationships that had ended before they had a chance to begin. She wondered if she would ever find the kind of love she longed for, or if she was destined to be alone.

Lost in thought, Maddie barely noticed the cyclist in front of her until she was almost upon him. He was wearing a bright yellow cycling top, the same shade as her Jeep. Something about him caught her eye, and for a moment, she watched him, intrigued by the way he seemed so at ease on the road, like he belonged there.

Her attention was quickly drawn back to the road as a car sped past her, cutting her off before swerving suddenly to avoid an oncoming truck. Maddie barely had time to react before the car that had just overtaken her veered off course, hitting the cyclist and sending him flying off his bike. She saw the scene in slow motion—the crash, the cyclist's body hitting the pavement, the screeching tires as Maddie tried to swerve out of the way—but it was too late.

The truck hit her Jeep head-on, the impact sending her vehicle careening off the road and into a ditch. The world spun around her as the Jeep tumbled, glass shattering, metal crumpling. When it finally came to a stop, Maddie was upside down, hanging from her seatbelt, her body twisted at an unnatural angle. She was barely conscious, her mind foggy and disoriented, the sound of sirens growing louder in the distance.

When the paramedics arrived, they worked quickly to free her from the wreckage, pulling her battered body from the mangled Jeep. She was rushed to the hospital, her life hanging by a thread, the same hospital where the cyclist had been taken just moments before.

As the doctors fought to save her, Maddie's thoughts drifted in and out, her mind flickering with memories of her life, her regrets, and the dreams that had never come true. She felt herself slipping away, the pain in her body fading as a strange peace settled over her.

In the operating room, the Grim Reaper appeared by her side, his presence both calming and inevitable. He looked down at her with gentle eyes, his voice soft as he spoke.

"Maddie," he said, "I know you've always wanted love. You've spent your life searching for it, hoping to find someone who would see you for who you are. Tonight, you were supposed to meet someone special, but fate had other plans. You were meant to meet the love of your life, but neither of you made it to where you were supposed to be tonight."

Maddie's mind, though hazy, tried to make sense of the Reaper's words. The sadness of what could have been weighed heavily on her heart. Was this man the one she had been waiting for all her life? Was he the answer to the questions that had haunted her for so long? The Reaper's words filled her with a deep longing, a sense of loss for something she never had the chance to experience.

"I know this isn't fair," the Reaper said gently, sensing her sorrow. "Your lives may have ended too soon, but that doesn't mean your souls can't find what they were meant to."

As the Reaper spoke, Maddie felt everything around her shift. The bright lights of the operating room faded into a soft, golden glow. The pain in her body disappeared, replaced by a warmth that enveloped her like a comforting embrace. She found herself standing in a beautiful place where the sky met the mountains in the distance.

There, standing in the glow of the sunset, was the man she had seen on the road—the cyclist in the yellow top. He looked at her with a kind smile, his eyes filled with the same mixture of curiosity and recognition that she felt.

The Reaper stepped forward, his voice a gentle whisper on the wind. He explained to them both that something happened on the day they were supposed to meet that prevented them from meeting. They were destined to meet at the wedding and spend the rest of their lives together.

"But fate had other plans. Although your lives ended too soon, your souls have found each other. You don't have to journey alone anymore. Together, your souls will continue on, in a place where time has no meaning, where love is eternal."

The Reaper gestured with a bony hand.

"Maddie, this is Jacob."

Echoes of the Past

Our lives are shaped by the memories we make and leave behind, guiding and connecting us across time.

The First Harvest

THE GRIM REAPER COULD appear wherever he wished, moving through the world unseen and untouched by the passage of time. Yet, sometimes, he liked to do things the way humans did, immersing himself briefly in their experiences, keeping himself entertained.

Tonight, he chose to appear in the dark, wooded field across from the hospital in the small town of Waxahachie, Texas. The night air was cool and calm, and the faint rustle of the leaves provided a gentle sound as he slowly made his way toward the hospital.

As he approached the hospital entrance, paramedics were unloading an unconscious old man from an ambulance parked a few feet away under the emergency room sign. It was not his time, and the Reaper wasn't there for him. The hospital scene was eerily quiet as visiting hours were coming to a close. The Reaper moved through the calmness, unnoticed.

The automatic doors at the main entrance did not sense him, but at a subtle wave of his hand they opened and then quickly closed behind him after he passed. A woman, sitting on a chair in the open area waiting room, noticed the doors opening without anyone there to trigger them. Too exhausted to give it a second thought, she shifted in her chair, crossed her arms, leaned her head on her husband's shoulder, and closed her eyes. The Reaper noticed her but was not concerned.

The Reaper continued down the hallway. He approached the elevators and waited patiently alongside a middle-aged man who was there to deliver flowers to a patient. The flowers were beautiful white roses. There was also a red balloon that read "Get Well Soon," and a small pink card adorned with a playful, glittery design was nestled among the blooms.

As he waited, a father and his young son, a boy of four wearing a black baseball cap with a rocket on it, a green sweatshirt, blue jeans, and black sneakers, walked up and stood next to him. In one hand, he held his father's hand, and in the other, the boy clutched a toy rocket like the one on his cap. Just as humans do, the Reaper found hand-holding comforting. It was not something he had ever done, nor was it something he planned on doing, but he liked seeing it, and found it to be a touching and meaningful gesture of affection, one that conveyed warmth and connection in a simple yet profound way.

The elevator doors opened, and the Reaper entered. The delivery guy stepped in and pushed the button for the second floor. The father and son stepped in next. The boy's finger went decisively to the button for the fourth floor and hovered there. He asked his father if he could push the button and then pressed it without waiting for an answer. The father laughed softly and nodded his head. As the elevator doors closed, they all shifted their eyes upwards to the slowly changing numbers on the display, and everyone was silent. Unbeknownst to all but the Reaper, he would soon return to visit the boy's baby brother, as well as the father of the girl receiving the balloon and flowers.

As they rode the elevator, the Reaper remained unnoticed. When the elevator stopped on the second floor, the flower-delivery man exited, leaving only the father and son. Now that the delivery man had exited, the boy's innocent chatter filled the small space. The elevator doors opened on the third floor. The Reaper stepped out and made his way to the end of the hall to room 307.

Grace lay in her bed, her frail body weakened by illness. Grace was only five years old, and she'd only experienced how grand life could be in brief moments. Most of her days had been confined to the four walls of different hospital rooms. Though this was her life, Grace also experienced kindness and love from everyone around her. She was constantly surrounded by caring doctors, nurses, family, friends, and most of all, her parents. Grace's parents sat by her side, their faces etched with sorrow and exhaustion. They knew she was departing this world right before their eyes, her time slipping away minute by minute.

As the Reaper entered the room, the air grew still. Grace, despite her condition, sensed him. Her eyes fluttered open, and she looked towards the shadowed corner where he stood. To her parents, she appeared to be lying completely still, with her eyes closed, and barely breathing.

Grace saw the Reaper clearly—a tall, cloaked figure with a calming aura. His skeletal face was softened by the glow of an otherworldly light radiating from his scythe. She did not feel fear; instead, she felt a deep sense of peace. To Grace's parents, the Reaper remained unseen.

The Reaper approached her bed and knelt beside her, his dark robe pooling around him like a protective shield. He did not speak with words but communicated through thoughts and feelings, a gentle whisper in her mind.

"Grace," he conveyed, "I am here to help you find peace. You have been very brave."

Grace looked into his dark eyes, seeing not the figure of death but a comforting guide. "Will my mommy and daddy be okay?" she asked, her voice weak but clear.

The Reaper nodded, projecting warmth and reassurance. "They will be sad, but they will find peace. You will watch over them, an angel, free from pain."

In that moment, Grace was strengthened and no longer felt pain. Its absence was unfamiliar to her. She sat up and shifted herself to the edge of the bed, and with a little wiggle, she made her way off the hospital bed where she had spent months trying to recover from her illness. She slipped her tiny feet into her favorite pink slippers that her parents had placed next to her bedside on the day she entered the hospital. She had worn them on the ambulance ride to the hospital, and she and her parents had agreed that she would wear them on her ride home.

Grace was ready. She knew her parents would be okay, and she was happy to know that she would always be with them.

As he watched Grace slip into her pink slippers, the Reaper's mind drifted back to a time long ago, to a desolate field where he had once found a boy lying still—a soul he was destined to guide, a task that had filled him with a deep sense of solemn responsibility. The boy's life had been cut short by his brother, and his innocent blood cried out from the earth. The Reaper had approached the boy, who lay still, his eyes wide open but unseeing. The innocence of the boy's soul, untainted by the complexities of human morality, had left an everlasting impression on the Reaper.

He compared that experience to now, taking the soul of an innocent child who had barely begun to understand the world. The weight of this task felt different, much deeper. He felt empathy, a rare flicker of emotion in his timeless existence.

The Reaper turned his attention back to Grace, who was now smiling faintly. "Will it hurt?" she asked. She wanted to prepare herself if it would.

"No," he assured her, his presence enveloping her in a cocoon of calm. "You will feel only peace."

Inspired by the connection he saw between the father and son in the elevator, he decided he would hold Grace's hand. He reached out to meet her tiny hand, and as their hands touched, it was just as if Grace was holding her father's hand. She could feel the warmth and softness of his skin, not skeletal bones. She was comforted by this and felt safe, just as she did with her father.

Together, they made their way toward the door, passing by her parents, who were lost in their grief. As Grace's soul departed, the Reaper extended his empathetic powers, ensuring that her parents found a sense of calm. They held each other tightly, their sobs turning into soft cries.

Grace's body lay lifeless, but her soul, now an angelic presence, watched over her parents with love and serenity. The Reaper waited a moment, his task complete. He had done more than just fulfilled his duty; he had granted a final act of kindness to the family, something that went beyond his usual responsibilities.

As they faded from the room, he reflected on the nature of innocence and the special care required in guiding such pure souls. He knew that while death was inevitable, the way he managed his role could bring comfort and peace, even in the darkest moments.

The Quilt

OLD MAN PETE WAS a man of few words, content with the quiet rhythm of his life. His days were filled with tending to his animals and crops, and his evenings were spent at home with his wife, in their modest farmhouse nestled among rolling hills of green. Pete had never been one for conversation, but he didn't need to be. The animals understood him, and his wife, gentle and loving, knew his heart without the need for words. The people in town often spoke kindly of Old Man Pete and his wife, though they knew little of the couple beyond their reputation for kindness and hard work.

Pete's farm was his world, and each creature in it was a part of him. The chickens, cows, goats, pigs, ducks, and his two horses were more than just livestock; they were his companions, his family. Every animal had a name, and Pete treated them as if they were his children. His two horses, in particular, held a special place in his heart. They had been with him for many years, loyal and steadfast, just like the man himself.

Pete's wife, though fragile in her old age, had always been a source of quiet strength. She spent her days quilting, her nimble fingers crafting beautiful blankets that she sold to the townspeople. Her quilts were renowned for their intricate designs, each one stitched with love and care. But as the years went by, her health began to decline. She had been ill when she was younger, and though she had survived, the illness had returned.

The doctors said there was nothing they could do this time. Pete knew her time was nearing, and it weighed heavily on him.

As her illness worsened, Pete took on the burden of the farm and caring for his wife. Every evening, after finishing his chores, he would pick flowers from their garden and bring them to her bedside, placing them in a small vase. He would sit with her, telling her about his day, about the animals and their antics—like how the mischievous goat had managed to sneak into the chicken coop again, causing a flurry of squawking hens. She would smile, her eyes bright with love, and listen to every word. Before she drifted off to sleep, he would kiss her gently on the forehead and tell her he loved her. It was their routine, one that gave them both comfort as the inevitable approached.

One afternoon, as Pete was working in the barn, he noticed one of his horses, the older of the two, lying down and refusing to get up. The horse had been with him for many years, and he knew that her time had come. Pete sat with her, stroking her mane, his heart heavy with sadness. He stayed with her through the night, speaking softly to her, just as he had always done. It was a painful reminder of the fragility of life, one that mirrored his wife's own fading strength.

The next evening, as the sun dipped below the horizon, Pete entered the barn and saw the horse breathing faintly. He knelt beside her, resting a hand on her side, feeling the shallow rise and fall of her chest. He knew this was it—the end. As the horse lay there, struggling for breath, the air around Pete grew still. A soft glow filled the barn, and he felt a presence beside him. He didn't need to turn around to know who it was.

The Grim Reaper stood quietly in the shadows, his scythe glimmering faintly in the fading light. Somehow, Pete wasn't afraid. There was a calmness in the Reaper's presence, an understanding that went beyond words.

Pete felt the weight of his grief lift, replaced by a quiet sense of peace. The Reaper, though silent, conveyed a message that Pete heard in his heart.

"You've done well," the feeling seemed to say. "Your care, your love—it hasn't gone unnoticed."

Pete's eyes filled with tears, but they were not tears of sorrow. The Reaper was here to guide his old friend, his beloved horse, to a place beyond pain and suffering. Pete nodded, his heart heavy yet full of acceptance. He sat with the horse until her final breath, the Reaper standing silently beside them. And when it was over, Pete felt a strange sense of relief. He knew his horse had gone to a place of peace, just as his wife would one day.

From that moment on, Pete found a new strength within himself. The Reaper's visit, though brief, had left him with a deep understanding that life was a cycle, and that all things must come to an end. But endings were not something to fear. There was comfort in knowing that those he loved would be cared for, even after they were gone.

As the months passed, Pete's wife grew weaker, but her spirit remained strong. She continued working on a quilt that she was determined to finish, her fingers never faltering despite her frailty. Pete knew how important it was to her to continue to work, and to finish this final project. He would sit by her bedside, telling her about the farm, about the animals, and about the memories they had shared over the years. He could see the love in her eyes, even as her body grew weaker.

And then, one day, the time came. Pete knew it before the doctors or anyone else. His wife's breathing had slowed, her eyes fluttering closed. He sat by her side, holding her hand, his heart heavy with the knowledge that she would soon be gone. But there was no fear, no panic. He had made his peace with it, just as he had with the loss of his horse.

As the sun set outside their window, the Reaper came again. His presence was gentle, as it had been before. This time, the Reaper moved closer to Pete, standing at the foot of the bed where Pete's wife lay. No words were spoken, but Pete felt the same sense of calm wash over him, just as he had before.

The love between Pete and his wife radiated through the room, and the Reaper, for a brief moment, was touched by it. For the first time in his long existence, the Reaper wondered what it might be like to live a life like theirs—one filled with love, companionship, and the quiet joy of growing old together. What would it be like to love someone so deeply and to be loved in return? To share a lifetime of memories, both simple and profound, and to know that, in the end, you had given and received all that truly mattered? His existence was bound by duty, not by the bonds of love. Yet, for a fleeting moment, he allowed himself to imagine it, to wonder if perhaps there was more to existence than the role he had always known.

But the Reaper did not linger on such thoughts. He had a task to fulfill.

Pete kissed his wife on the forehead, his voice breaking as he whispered, "I love you. I'll see you again." He watched as the Reaper gently took her soul, guiding her to the place where she would wait for him. There was no pain, no suffering—only peace. Pete's heart ached, but he was calm. He knew she was in good hands, and that one day, they would be reunited.

The townspeople came together to help Pete lay his wife to rest. They had always admired the couple, their simple yet meaningful life. After the service, as Pete returned to their home to gather her things, he found the quilt she had been working on, neatly folded in the chest where she had always kept her sewing supplies. And next to it, a letter addressed to him.

With trembling hands, Pete opened the letter and began to read.

My dearest Pete,

I've been working on this quilt for you, for us, for the life we've shared. Each square holds a hand-stitched flower from our garden, a reflection of the flowers you've picked for me every day. They've brought me so much joy over the years, just as you have. I've embroidered them here, so that when I'm gone, you'll have something to help you remember our simple, beautiful life together.

Thank you for all the love you've given me, for the wonderful years we've spent together. I've never needed more than your love to be happy. You made me feel special every day, in ways you'll never know. Our life has been filled with love, and I wouldn't change a single moment.

This isn't goodbye, my love. I'll be waiting for you in a place where there's no pain, no suffering—just peace. Until we meet again, know that I'll always be with you, in every flower you pick, in every memory we've shared. Please, continue to pick flowers for me, just as you always have, and place them in the vase on the bedside table. As you do, think of me, as I'll be there with you each night, just as I was before. Let their beauty fill our room and let them remind you of the love we've shared and the life we built together.

With all my love, now and always, E.

Tears filled Pete's eyes as he clutched the letter to his chest. He ran his hands over the quilt, each flower a reminder of the love they had shared.

As he held the quilt, Pete felt a sense of comfort, as though she were still beside him, her hand resting gently in his. The softness of the fabric brought him solace, much like her touch had during their many years together. It was a piece of her, a tangible expression of the love that had bound them together for so long.

As Pete laid the quilt across their bed, he felt a warmth in his heart, knowing that his wife's love would be with him always. And though he was alone now, he knew that she was waiting for him, just as she had promised. Every evening, as he had done for so many years, Pete continued to pick flowers from their garden, bringing them to the vase on the bedside table. Though she was gone, he still chose the brightest and most beautiful blooms, knowing she would have loved them. And each night, as he drifted off to sleep, he held the quilt close, just as he had held her close for so many years, finding peace in the memories of their life together and comfort in the thought that she was never truly far away.

The Gift

BETH SAT IN HER favorite chair, with a knitted blanket she'd made draped over her legs as she stared out of a window. She looked onto a beautiful, serene lake. Tall trees framed the water, with snowcapped mountains standing proudly in the distance. The scene was tranquil, she felt as if the world beyond the window had paused just for her.

Her mind wandered, drifting into memories. Each one came to her gently, like a replay from the past, but with a vividness that made it feel as though she was living them again, and not for the first time. They all seemed familiar, as if they were memories of a life once lived.

Beth was a mother of four—two sons and two daughters. The eldest were twin girls, followed by her two boys. She had watched each of her children grow, nurturing their dreams as they grew. She had been there for the joys of their weddings, the births of her grandchildren, and the small, everyday moments that bound their lives together. She felt the warmth of these memories, the laughter of her grandchildren, her pride as a mother, and the bittersweet pain of watching her children face their own challenges.

Beth thought about the devastating loss of her beloved husband. One morning, she had awoken to find him lying beside her, lifeless. The shock of that moment never fully left her. She hadn't had the chance to say goodbye, and that absence of closure stayed with her for decades. But even as she mourned, she continued to live, finding solace in her children, her friends, and the memories of the life she had shared with the man she loved. Every so often, she would find herself lost in thoughts of him, feeling the ache of his absence and the enduring love she still held for him.

Beth's life had been filled with friends, and she was never truly alone. One particular friend came to mind as she sat by the window. This friend had taken care of her when she needed it most. She often confided in Beth, pouring out her troubles while Beth listened patiently, offering words of comfort and support. She remembered those conversations clearly—how she had tried to be a source of strength, even when it seemed her words went unheard. But now, as she recalled these moments, she felt something different. She could feel the love and gratitude of her friend, who knelt beside her, thanking her, tears in her eyes, for always being there. Beth tried to console her but the tears were unstoppable and Beth felt helpless. She reached out, as if to comfort her friend once more, and as she did, the world around her shifted.

Suddenly, Beth found herself with someone, not alone, but beside a tall figure cloaked in shadows—the Grim Reaper. The realization washed over her slowly, like the rising tide, but it did not bring fear. Instead, there was a calm acceptance, a sense that she was exactly where she was meant to be.

The Reaper's voice was gentle as he spoke. "Beth, I wanted you to experience the parts of your life that you missed. The human body is fragile, and as it declines, it takes with it precious moments and your memories. Your mind began to fail you, robbing you of many beautiful moments. I wanted you to feel them, to live them fully, before you continued on your journey. This is my gift to you."

Beth listened, understanding now that the memories she had been reliving were not just recollections, but experiences granted to her by the

Reaper—a chance to reclaim what the illness had stolen from her. Gratitude welled up within her, and she looked at the Reaper with eyes full of thanks. "Thank you," she whispered, her voice filled with emotion.

The Reaper nodded. "I'm not done yet, Beth."

As he spoke, the sky around them darkened briefly, only to brighten again, revealing a silhouette standing in the distance. The figure was tall, with broad shoulders, and though his face remained in shadow, Beth knew instantly who it was. Her heart leaped as she recognized the man she had loved and lost.

"My love," she breathed, tears filling her eyes. "You didn't say goodbye. I have missed you so."

Her husband stepped into the light, a soft smile on his face. "I didn't say goodbye because I knew I would see you again. I've been here, watching over you, waiting for this moment. Your memories are now mine as well. I've seen your life, our children's lives, and the lives of our grandchildren. We will watch them together now, and we will live on through their memories."

Beth walked toward him, feeling the years of separation melt away. She reached out, and he took her hand, his touch warm and familiar. Together, they walked into the light, leaving the world behind.

The Reaper watched them go, feeling the strength of their love, before he faded into the shadows. His work was done.

Shadows of Understanding

When curiosity meets mortality, answers are found in the silence between life and death.

The Presence in the Shadows

IN A QUIET, DIMLY lit room, the air seemed to grow heavier, as if burdened by an unseen weight. For John, this heaviness was more than just a feeling: it was a presence. He could sense it—the unmistakable chill of the Grim Reaper in the room.

He sat still in his beloved wingback chair, his eyes attentively scanning the dusty volumes and mementos from a life well-lived that filled his study. The clock on the wall ticked steadily, each second tapping against the silence. Outside, the world continued its usual ebb and flow, but here, within these four walls, time seemed to slow, each tick amplifying the sense of an unseen observer.

It was as if the shadows themselves had come alive. His eyes swept the dark room, trying to pinpoint the source of his unease.

His gaze fell on a dimly lit corner of the room, its shadows too deep for the antique lamp—perched on a Queen Anne table—to brighten. There, between the table and an old armchair, he thought he saw a figure—a silhouette cloaked in darkness. His heart raced, but he forced himself to remain calm. This was not the first time he had sensed something otherworldly—his sensitivity to the supernatural had always unsettled and fascinated him—but it was the first time the presence felt so ... personal.

It intrigued the Reaper that John could discern his presence. The living could not normally detect him unless they were on the brink of death. Yet, here was John, very much alive, staring directly at him. He hadn't come to collect John's soul—not yet. He'd come to answer John's questions.

John, feeling a strange mix of fear and curiosity, decided to speak. "I know you're there," he said, his voice steady despite the tremor in his hands. "I don't know why, but I can feel you. Why are you here?"

The Reaper, unused to such direct interaction with the living, remained silent. He caused a wave of calm to wash over John, a silent assurance that he meant no harm and at the same time confirming to John that he was indeed there. John felt the change in the air, the heaviness lifting slightly, replaced by an inexplicable sense of peace.

The Reaper stood silently, his presence a blend of the eternal and the ephemeral. Eternal because he had existed since the dawn of life. Time did not bind him. He had witnessed the rise and fall of countless civilizations and was tied to the endless cycle of life and death. His ephemeral nature allowed him to be present in the fleeting moments of each individual's final breath. His existence was defined by his duty—to collect the souls of the deceased and guide them to the afterlife. This role was not one of malice but of solemn responsibility, ensuring the balance of the universe was maintained.

John wondered why the Reaper had come. He felt sure that the presence he felt was not here to take him. Didn't he then have somewhere else to be? John did not know about the Reaper's many abilities, like the power to manipulate time, enabling him to be present at countless deaths simultaneously. He was able to operate in a dimension where time was fluid, each moment containing infinite smaller ones. He could slow it down or speed it up as needed. Every being with a soul felt his unique, undivided presence.

He could appear wherever he wished, sometimes choosing to experience interactions in their entirety, even as he fulfilled his duty. Tonight, he chose to visit John. The minutes he spent visiting John were fractal moments of time and he was exactly where he needed to be.

John thought about the history of the Grim Reaper. Different cultures and religions had depicted him in various ways, but all shared the common theme of a being who guides souls to the afterlife. In some traditions, he was seen as a dark and menacing figure, while in others, he was seen as a compassionate guide.

John couldn't help himself. "Do you collect more than just human souls?" he asked, his voice barely above a whisper.

The Reaper's mind flickered with the countless souls he had guided—humans, animals, even ancient beings forgotten by time. He was there to guide each one to the next chapter.

John closed his eyes, allowing his other senses to take over. He could almost see the glowing threads of life the Reaper perceived, each one with its unique essence. He felt the faint traces of emotions—hope, fear, love, and despair, intermingling in the room.

He opened his eyes and whispered, "Thank you." He wasn't entirely sure why he said it, but it felt right. He was grateful for the silent guardian of souls, the one who ensured the cycle of life and death remained unbroken.

Satisfied that their brief connection had imparted a sliver of understanding, the Reaper began to withdraw. He had other souls to attend to, other lives to guide. As his presence faded, the room grew lighter, the shadows retreating to their usual places.

John felt the change, the return of normalcy. Yet, he knew that his life had been touched by something profound. He would never forget the night he sensed the presence in the shadows, the silent guardian who had, for a moment, bridged the gap between life and death to answer his question.

Before this encounter, John had feared death, as most humans do. But now, after feeling the Reaper's presence, he found his fear had diminished. He understood that death was not something to dread but a part of the natural cycle. This realization allowed him to enjoy life more fully, focusing on living rather than the inevitable end.

John continued his life with a renewed sense of purpose and peace, knowing that when his time came, he would be guided by the same calm presence he had felt that night. The Grim Reaper, ever vigilant, returned to his eternal duty, forever watching over the fragile balance of existence.

The Visit

JOHN SAT IN THE dimly lit room, his eyes fixed on the fragile figure lying in the bed before him. His father, a man who had once been full of life and strength, was now a shadow of his former self. Age had claimed his vitality, leaving him frail and weak, each breath a laborious effort. John knew that the end was near; he could feel it in the stillness of the room, in the way time seemed to stretch and contract all at once.

As he sat there, keeping vigil over his father's final moments, a familiar sensation washed over him—a cold, tingling presence that seemed to seep into the very air around him. John didn't need to look up to know who had arrived. He had felt this presence once before, years ago, in his study. The memory of that night came flooding back to him—the night when the Grim Reaper had visited him, answering his unspoken questions, confirming the reality of his existence.

Without turning his gaze from his father, John spoke softly, a slight smile tugging at the corners of his lips. "I knew you'd come back," he said, his voice steady despite the emotion that threatened to choke him. "I felt you the moment you entered the room."

There was no reply, but John didn't need one. He could sense the Reaper's acknowledgment, a silent affirmation that hung in the air between them.

"It's been a long time," John continued, his tone conversational, as if he were speaking to an old friend. "I've often wondered when I might see you again. I suppose I should have expected it would be under these circumstances."

He finally turned his head, his eyes meeting the dark, shadowed figure standing at the foot of his father's bed. The Reaper's form was as John remembered—cloaked in darkness, a scythe held in his bony hand, his face obscured by the deep hood of his robe. Despite the grim appearance, John felt no fear, only a deep, abiding curiosity.

"You're here for my father," John said, more a statement than a question. The Reaper inclined his head ever so slightly, the movement almost imperceptible.

John nodded in understanding. "He's lived a good life, you know. A long, fulfilling life. I suppose it's only natural that you'd come for him now."

There was a brief silence, the only sound in the room the faint, labored breathing of John's father. John took a deep breath, knowing that his time with the Reaper was limited, but determined to make the most of it.

"Since you're here," John began, his voice thoughtful, "I have to ask ... what is it like for you? Do you ever grow weary of this duty? Of guiding souls from this world to the next?"

The Reaper didn't answer in words, but John felt the response in his mind—a deep, resonant sense of duty, of purpose that transcended weariness or emotion. The Reaper was neither burdened nor indifferent; he simply was, a constant presence in the cycle of life and death, fulfilling a role that had always existed and always would.

John nodded slowly, absorbing the unspoken reply. "I see," he said softly. "You're not driven by the things that drive us—fear, love, sorrow. You're ... beyond those things."

The Reaper's silence spoke volumes, confirming John's understanding. He had suspected as much during their first encounter, but now he knew for certain. The Reaper was an entity unto himself, a being whose existence was intertwined with life and death.

"Do you remember our last conversation?" John asked, a slight smile playing on his lips. "I asked you if you collected more than just human souls, and you confirmed it. Animals, too, and perhaps other beings beyond our comprehension."

Again, there was no verbal response, but John felt the Reaper's acknowledgment. He remembered their previous encounter vividly, the way it had changed his perspective on life and death, how it had left him with a sense of peace he had never known before.

"Do you ever question your role?" John continued, his curiosity getting the better of him. "Do you ever wonder why it has to be this way? Why there must be an end to everything?"

This time, the Reaper's presence shifted slightly, a subtle change in the air that John interpreted as contemplation. He sensed that the Reaper did not dwell on such questions, that his existence was one of acceptance and fulfillment of his role. There was no need to question the natural order of things; it simply was.

John sighed, a bittersweet smile crossing his face. "I suppose it's not your place to question it. You are what you are. And in a way, that's a comfort, isn't it? Knowing that some things are beyond our control, beyond our understanding."

He paused, glancing down at his father, whose breaths were growing weaker, more infrequent. "You'll take good care of him, won't you?" John asked, his voice almost pleading. "He deserves peace after everything he's done, after the life he's lived."

The Reaper remained silent, but John felt a sense of reassurance, a promise that his father's soul would be guided gently to the next stage of its journey.

John took a deep breath, feeling the weight of the moment settling over him. "I'm not afraid for him," he said quietly. "I know he's in good hands."

There was a long silence, during which John's father took his last breath. The room grew still, the air heavy with the finality of the moment. John closed his eyes, a single tear slipping down his cheek, not out of sorrow, but out of gratitude for the life his father had lived and the peace he now hoped his father would find.

When he opened his eyes again, the Reaper was gone, and John's father lay still, a peaceful expression on his face. The room was quiet, the presence of the Reaper lingering only in John's memory.

John sat in silence for a long time, processing everything that had just happened. He felt a deep sense of calm, much like the one he had experienced during his first encounter with the Reaper. The knowledge that his father had been gently guided to the next life brought him comfort, easing the pain of his loss.

As he rose from his chair and looked down at his father's lifeless form, John felt a sense of closure. The Reaper had come, just as he knew he would, and had answered the questions that lingered in John's heart.

As he left the room, John whispered a quiet farewell to his father, and though he knew it might be years before he saw the Reaper again, he also knew that when that time came, he would welcome it. The Reaper was not an enemy, but a guide—a presence in the shadows who offered understanding and peace in the face of life's greatest mystery.

Ripples of Justice

Actions ripple outward, bringing fairness and understanding to the stories of our lives.

Between Worlds

A HEAVY MIST BLANKETED the night, shrouding the alley in darkness and an eerie, damp stillness. The only sound was the faint, rhythmic drip of water from a broken pipe. A woman stumbled into the alley, her steps unsteady as if drawn by an unseen force. From the darkness, two glowing red eyes emerged, watching her with predatory intent.

Count Dracula stepped forward, his silhouette sharp against the faint moonlight. His movements were fluid, almost hypnotic, as he closed the distance between them. The woman gasped, but before she could scream, his fangs sank into her neck. Warm, crimson life flowed into him, renewing his strength and feeding his endless hunger. He drank deeply, indifferent to her quiet whimper and fading heartbeat.

A voice interrupted the macabre feast, chilling and resonant, like a storm rolling over a desolate plain. "Enough."

Dracula froze, the woman's lifeless body slipping from his grasp. He turned to face the speaker. Standing at the end of the alley was a figure cloaked in shadow, wielding a scythe that seemed to shimmer with otherworldly energy. The Grim Reaper.

"You," Dracula hissed, wiping his lips as though caught in an unspeakable act.

The Reaper's eyes, though hidden, burned with a fury that made the air around them heavy. "I have come for her soul, as I have countless others you've stolen from this world."

Dracula's lip curled into a sneer. "And what of it? They are but fleeting mortals. Their lives are brief, insignificant. I endure."

The Reaper's grip on his scythe tightened. "You endure at a cost. Their cost." He stepped closer, the fog parting like a curtain before him. "Do you even comprehend the weight of what you've done? The lives you've destroyed for your insatiable thirst?"

Dracula smirked, but his arrogance faltered under the Reaper's gaze. "They are food, nothing more."

The Reaper raised a skeletal hand, pointing at Dracula. "Then let us see what 'food' has cost the world." With a wave of his hand, the alley dissolved into a whirlwind of shadows and light, pulling Dracula into a vortex of memories—not his own, but those of his victims.

Dracula found himself in a small, candlelit home. A child lay in bed, her face pale, her tiny chest barely rising. Her mother knelt beside her, tears streaming down her face as she whispered prayers. The specter of her father stood apart, shoulders hunched, and stared at an empty chair by the fire.

Dracula understood what he was seeing. He had taken the father's life months before, leaving the family to fend for themselves. Without the father's income, they had fallen into poverty, and now the child was dying of an illness they could no longer afford to treat.

An overwhelming force surged through Dracula as the Reaper's presence enveloped him, heavy and unyielding. It wasn't a voice, but a profound, unspoken command that echoed in his mind: *You will not merely witness, Count. You will feel what they felt.* Dracula's body stiffened as an unnatural force gripped him, pulling him deeper into the memory. The mother's despair clutched at his heart, the father's terror coursed through his veins, and the child's loneliness wrapped around him like a suffocating fog. It was unbearable.

The scene shifted to a forest. A wolf lay motionless on the ground, its fur matted with blood. Its mate stood nearby, howling mournfully. Dracula remembered this too—he had killed the wolf in a moment of sport, drinking its blood to stave off hunger when human prey was scarce.

The Reaper's presence resonated. "Their bond was as deep as any human's. You shattered it for your amusement."

Dracula's knees buckled as the mate's grief pierced him like a blade. He could feel the wolf's pain—a hollow, consuming sorrow that reverberated through his very being. The Reaper's power amplified the emotions, leaving Dracula gasping for breath. "Stop this!" he growled, but the Reaper remained unmoved.

Now he stood in a bustling city square, watching as a man collapsed in the street. Passersby ignored him, thinking him drunk. Dracula knew better. He had drained the man just hours earlier, leaving him too weak to live but not dead enough to warrant immediate attention.

The man's soul hovered nearby, confused and terrified, before the Reaper appeared to guide him. His voice was stern. "Your time was stolen, and with it, the dreams you had yet to fulfill."

Dracula doubled over as the man's despair crashed over him like a tidal wave. He saw flashes of the man's life—an unfinished love, the unspoken words he would never share, the future stolen from him in an instant. Each broken dream ripped through Dracula's mind like shards of glass. "Enough!" Dracula hissed, his voice cracking under the weight of the emotions. "I cannot bear it."

Dracula and the Reaper stood once again in the alley. The woman's body lay at their feet, her soul now glowing faintly in the Reaper's grasp. Dracula trembled, his usual arrogance replaced by a hollow shame.

"You ... you've made your point," Dracula muttered, his voice unsteady.

The Reaper stepped closer, towering over the vampire. "Have I? Do you now understand the weight of what you've done? The lives you've stolen, the ripples of pain you've caused?"

Dracula's fists clenched. "I did what I had to do to survive."

The Reaper's anger flared. "Survive? You have taken what was never yours to claim. You, who were once human, have forgotten the sanctity of life. You are a coward, hiding behind your curse to justify your atrocities."

Dracula's crimson eyes burned with defiance, but the raw memories and emotions coursing through him made his voice falter. For the first time in centuries, he felt the faintest stirrings of compassion, a crack in the armor of his self-serving existence. His shoulders sagged under the weight of the pain the Reaper had forced him to carry.

The Reaper leaned in, his presence looming, an unspoken warning pressing into Dracula's mind. "I am not here for your soul, Count. Not yet. But one day, I will come for you, and there will be no escape. No shadows to hide in, no lives to steal. You will face the weight of eternity and answer for every life you have taken."

Dracula's form wavered, his pride and shame battling within him. Finally, he stepped back into the shadows. "One day," he echoed, the words ringing hollowly in the vampire's mind.

The Reaper watched as Dracula disappeared into the night, leaving only the faint scent of blood and despair. He turned to the woman's soul, now glowing brighter in his grasp. With a solemn nod, he guided her into the beyond, his scythe glinting in the pale moonlight.

As he faded into the ether, the Reaper's presence lingered in the air. "Life is precious, even to the damned."

The Price of Deception

MAURA WAS A MASTER of illusion.

In her sixties, she lacked any extraordinary good looks—and in fact had never been a beauty—yet her talent for weaving charm and manipulation into every interaction had made her irresistible to the lonely hearts of the elderly for many years.

She had perfected the art of assuming roles that would endear her to men seeking companionship. Caretaker, housekeeper, personal assistant—whatever was needed to burrow into their lives and secure her position as their partner, wife, confidante and, ultimately, their beneficiary.

Her victims were always older men, yearning for the warmth of affection they once knew or seeking a mistress to revive their faded desires. Maura would find these men, study their needs, and craft herself into whatever persona would make them believe she was their ideal companion. They would pour their hearts, their finances, and their futures into her care, only to find themselves ensnared in her web of deceit.

One by one, Maura's victims would succumb to their inevitable demise. Each time, the Grim Reaper, cloaked in his dark, hooded robe, would appear beside their deathbeds, shaking his head in silent disappointment. He watched as she amassed wealth and manipulated her way into the fortunes of those she preyed upon, knowing full well that her day of reckoning was drawing closer.

With her ill-gotten wealth, Maura built a life of luxury. One of her proudest acquisitions was a sleek, extravagant yacht—a gift she convinced one of her wealthiest victims to leave her in his will. She reveled in the indulgences her schemes afforded her, spending her days sailing the open sea, basking in the illusion of her triumph.

The climax of her story came on a solo sailing trip. The open sea, so often a symbol of freedom, became the stage for her final moments. As she lounged on the deck, sipping champagne and relishing the spoils of her deception, the weather began to deteriorate. The once calm waters turned turbulent, and dark clouds gathered ominously. Maura looked up, her heart racing as she saw the Grim Reaper emerging from the storm.

The Reaper's entrance was nothing short of dramatic. His presence intensified the storm, his dark robe billowing like a shroud of impending doom. His scythe, gleaming in the flashes of lightning, seemed to command the very winds and waves to churn with greater fury. The storm raged around her, the yacht tossed violently by the angry sea.

On the deck, Maura clung to the railing, her fear palpable. Her face was a mask of terror as she saw the Reaper drawing closer, his form growing larger and more menacing with each passing moment. She could feel the weight of her actions bearing down on her as the storm surged.

In a sudden, violent lurch, Maura was thrown overboard, her screams swallowed by the howling wind. She flailed desperately in the churning water, her attempts to swim futile against the powerful currents. As the Reaper watched from above, his voice echoed in her mind.

"Maura," he intoned with a chilling calmness, "the struggle you now endure, the feeling of drowning and gasping for air—this is the despair you inflicted upon others. You left many in their darkest moments, alone and bereft. Your actions have brought you to this point. The weight of your wrongs has finally caught up with you."

As Maura's strength waned, her last breaths came in ragged gasps. The Reaper reached out, his scythe slicing through the storm's fury as he collected her soul. The water calmed instantly as Maura's final moments faded into the darkness.

With her soul now in his grasp, the Grim Reaper disappeared into the void, leaving behind the tempest that had marked the end of Maura's manipulative life. The storm receded, leaving only the dark waters and the silence of finality. The path to the next existence was shrouded in darkness, a stark contrast to the life of deceit Maura had lived.

As the Reaper and Maura's soul vanished into the abyss, the echoes of her manipulative schemes and the consequences they wrought were left to linger in the shadows, a reminder of the price of deception.

The Timekeeper

THE TOWN OF SAN Jacinto was a simple place, located in a valley where time moved as gently as the creek that ran through its heart. With a population of barely eighty, every soul in San Jacinto bore the burden of a vital role. There was the schoolteacher who taught the children, the blacksmith who kept the people's tools sharp, and the preacher who filled their hearts with faith. Many others played equally essential parts—tending to the land, mending the sick, running the bustling general store, and ensuring homes and barns stood strong against the wind's fury. And then there was Winston, the town's clockmaker, whose steady hands and precise craft ensured that time itself remained a constant thread in the lives of them all.

Winston was more than just a man who repaired timepieces. He was the heartbeat of San Jacinto. His shop, a cozy nook filled with the gentle tick of pendulums and the hum of gears, was the lifeline for the town. The church bell relied on his skill, as did the town square clock that marked their days. People came to him not just for the clocks but for advice, for wisdom, for reassurance that time itself would always march forward.

But time had turned cruel on Winston. The persistent cough, the deep ache in his bones—he knew what it meant. The doctor confirmed his fears but swore to secrecy. The town could not know. Winston, the man who kept their lives ticking smoothly, was dying.

Winston resolved to find a replacement, someone who could carry the responsibility of his craft. But how could he do so without alarming the town? He began watching people carefully, testing their skills subtly, gauging their interest. He asked the blacksmith's apprentice about gears. He chatted with the schoolteacher about the mechanics of the town's bell. Yet no one seemed to have the knack for his delicate craft.

One evening, as a soft rain fell on the town, a stranger arrived. The man, gaunt and shadowed by the flickering lantern light, introduced himself as a traveler passing through. He stopped by Winston's shop to have a pocket watch repaired. Knowing the man was a traveler and would be gone the next day, Winston felt safe confiding in him. "You must have seen so many places in your travels," Winston said as he worked. "This town is my entire life. The people here depend on me, and I ..." He hesitated, coughing. "I'm looking for someone to carry on my work when I'm gone. But that someone has yet to appear."

The stranger's gaze sharpened as he listened, his expression thoughtful yet unreadable. "You've built something irreplaceable here," the man said. "It would be a shame for it to crumble when you're gone." Winston nodded, his heart heavy.

That night, the stranger made his decision. He saw an opportunity to create a new life for himself. If Winston were gone, he could claim to be a distant relative, arriving just in time to help the town. No one would suspect him of foul play, and the town's gratitude would make his lie all the easier to believe.

The next evening, the stranger returned, carrying a flask. "For your hospitality," he said, holding it out to Winston. "A gift from my travels. A rare, spiced liquor you won't find anywhere else." Winston hesitated but eventually accepted, touched by the gesture. As they shared a toast,

Winston felt the burn of the drink warming him, but soon, his vision blurred, and he stumbled, collapsing onto the floor of his shop.

The poison worked quickly. Winston collapsed on the floor of his shop, the stranger slipping away into the night. As darkness encroached, Winston felt his heartbeat slowing, his breath faltering.

The room grew eerily still. The faint ticking of clocks faded into silence, and the shadows in the corners of the shop seemed to deepen and stretch. A cold, gentle wind swept through, carrying with it the faint scent of lavender and something ancient, something Winston could not name.

The Grim Reaper appeared. The Reaper was neither skeletal nor terrifying. Emerging from the shadows, his form seemed to coalesce like smoke drawn into being. His movements were slow, deliberate, and unnaturally quiet, as if the very air held its breath. Cloaked in the soft shadows of the room, Winston felt no fear. There were no words, only a quiet understanding that flowed between them.

Finally, the Reaper's voice, soft and resonant, broke the silence. "It is not your time," he said, the words carrying a strange, undeniable weight. "You will wake. The illness will claim you one day, but not yet. There is more for you to do."

The pain dulled, the shadows deepened, and Winston closed his eyes.

When he awoke, sunlight streamed through the shop window. Flowers, cards, and notes surrounded him. The townsfolk had rallied together, their love for him evident in every gesture.

The sheriff arrived later that day with news: the stranger had been caught. The doctor, tending to Winston during his recovery, had revealed the truth. Not only had the doctor known of Winston's illness, but he had also discovered the traces of poison in Winston's body. With this evidence, the sheriff apprehended the traveler before he could slip away from town, unraveling his false story of being a relative.

What surprised Winston most was his shop. Despite his absence, the clocks had been wound, repairs had been made, and orders had been filled. The townsfolk had stepped in, ensuring that life in San Jacinto continued uninterrupted. Winston, who had always worried that the town depended on him too much, saw now how much they depended on each other.

Winston returned to work, his body weaker but his heart lighter. He no longer searched for a replacement, for he understood now that life was not about holding the world together alone. It was about the bonds between people, the way they lifted each other when the weight grew too heavy.

Weeks passed, and Winston grew weaker still. The day came when he closed his eyes, knowing it was the end. His heart was full, and he was ready. When he opened his eyes again, he was in the Reaper's realm. The Reaper stood before him, an unspoken warmth radiating from his silent form.

The Reaper's message was clear: "Your work is done. The town will endure. Come now, there is more for you beyond."

With a peaceful smile, Winston followed the Reaper into the light of his next existence.

The Hunt

THE FOREST WAS STILL that morning, the air crisp and filled with the earthy scent of pine. The soft rustling of leaves in the gentle breeze and the occasional call of a distant bird were the only sounds. Luke, a seasoned hunter, crouched quietly, his eyes fixed on the deer grazing in a small clearing ahead. His heart beat steadily in his chest, a familiar rush of adrenaline surging through him as he carefully lined up his shot. The world seemed to narrow down to just him and the deer, the rest of the forest fading into the background.

Luke had been hunting for years, drawn to the quiet challenge of tracking animals through the wilderness. He loved the solitude, the way the forest enveloped him, making him feel like a part of something ancient and enduring. Today, he was out with a group of friends, but in this moment, it was just him and the deer. He could feel the weight of the rifle in his hands, the tension in his muscles as he prepared to pull the trigger.

But as he watched the deer, something caught his attention out of the corner of his eye. Two small shapes, barely visible through the underbrush, moved cautiously toward the deer. Luke's breath caught as he recognized them—grizzly cubs, still young, exploring the world under the watchful eye of their mother, who was no doubt nearby.

Luke hesitated, torn between the excitement of the hunt and the knowledge that he was now in dangerous territory. Where there were cubs, a protective mother was never far behind.

But the thrill of the hunt had him in its grip. Ignoring his better judgement, he decided to take the shot. His finger tightened on the trigger.

The crack of the rifle echoed through the trees, startling the deer, which bolted into the dense foliage. The cubs, frightened by the sudden noise, began to cry out, their small voices echoing through the forest. Luke's heart raced as he scanned the trees, searching for the mother bear. He could hear the cubs crashing through the underbrush, their panic growing with each passing second.

Then he saw her—a massive grizzly, emerging from the shadows with a furious roar. She charged toward him, a blur of power and fury, her protective instincts driving her forward. Luke's training fled in that moment, replaced by sheer panic. Instead of standing his ground, he turned and ran, his heart pounding in his ears as he tried to escape the inevitable.

The bear was on him in an instant, her powerful legs propelling her across the ground faster than any human could hope to run. Luke felt the earth tremble beneath her weight. He could hear her breathing, a deep, rumbling sound that grew louder as she closed the distance between them. Then, with a swipe of her paw, she knocked him to the ground, her claws tearing through his clothes and into his flesh.

Pain shot through Luke's body as he hit the ground, the world spinning around him. The bear was on top of him now, her massive form blocking out the sky. He could feel the heat of her body, the wildness of her breath as she mauled him, driven by the need to protect her cubs. His thoughts became a jumble of fear and regret as he lay there, unable to move, his life slipping away.

Luke heard the sharp crack of a gunshot, and felt a jolt go through the bear's body. He lay there, gasping for breath, his vision dimming as he struggled to stay conscious. A second shot rang out, louder and closer this time, and he felt the weight of the bear slide off him. The ground shook as the bear collapsed beside him, her life ending as abruptly as his had nearly been taken. In the sudden stillness, Luke could hear the leaves rustling softly.

His friends rushed to his side, their voices filled with concern as they tried to keep him awake. But their words were fading, replaced by a growing darkness that began to envelop him. As he lay there, caught between life and death, a strange calmness settled over him. The light around him dimmed, and then he saw it—a dark figure emerging from the shadows, draped in a flowing black robe, holding a scythe that seemed to absorb the light around it.

The figure approached him slowly. Luke felt a strange sense of peace, as if he had been expecting this moment all along.

The Reaper stood silently before Luke, his face hidden beneath the hood of his robe. No words were spoken, yet Luke understood why he was there. The Reaper reached out, and with a wave of his hand, the scene around them changed. The forest reappeared, but this time, Luke saw the lifeless form of the grizzly bear lying beside him, her spirit hovering above her body, just as his was.

The bear's spirit was confused and distraught, her thoughts filled with worry for her cubs. Luke could feel her fear, her desperation to protect them even in death. The Reaper stood between them, silent but powerful, and in that moment, Luke understood that their fates were linked.

Through the Reaper's presence, Luke and the bear were able to communicate, to understand each other's pain. The bear wanted to know why Luke had threatened her cubs, why he had brought such danger into their lives. Luke, filled with remorse, tried to explain that it wasn't her cubs he had been hunting. He had been after the deer, not realizing the consequences of his actions.

As they stood there, connected by the Reaper's power, time in the world of the living continued to move forward. Luke's wife and sons mourned his loss, their grief deep and painful. The bear's cubs, lost and alone, wandered the forest, searching for their mother. They were too young to survive on their own, and soon, hunger and fear drove them to the edge of the forest, where the trees gave way to open fields and the outskirts of town, where houses dotted the landscape, and the sounds of life echoed from the human world.

There, the cubs encountered Luke's sons, who were playing in a field near their home. The boys, grieving the loss of their father, felt a strange connection to the cubs, who were equally lost and alone. Instead of fearing the animals, the boys saw in them a reflection of their own pain. They approached the cubs with kindness, offering food and comfort, and the bond between them began.

The cubs, who had known only fear and distress since their mother's death, began to trust the boys, finding in them the care and protection they had lost.

The boys, feeling a natural connection to the orphaned cubs, spent more time with them, bringing them food and playing with them in the fields at the edge of the forest. Their mother noticed the bond between her sons and the cubs. Though her heart was still heavy with the loss of her husband, she couldn't deny the innocence and gentle nature of the young bears.

Gradually, the cubs became a part of their lives. The mother, with a heart full of empathy, found herself caring for the cubs just as much as her sons did. She would watch over them as they played together, ensuring they were safe. The boys treated the cubs like family, and soon, an even deeper bond formed between the two brothers and the bear cubs, a bond that only grew stronger as the days turned into years. The mother, too, found solace in caring for the cubs, her own way of healing from the tragedy they had all endured.

As the years passed, the boys and the cubs grew up together, their lives connected in a way that neither could have imagined. The boys, who had once dreamed of following in their father's footsteps as hunters, found that their experiences with the cubs had changed them. They no longer saw animals as prey, but as beings deserving of care and respect. The cubs, who had once been wild and frightened, became gentle and trusting, a testament to the power of love and compassion.

Back in the ethereal realm, the Reaper allowed Luke and the bear to witness the lives they had left behind. They watched as the boys and the cubs grew up together, their bond unbreakable, their lives filled with the love and friendship that had transcended species. Luke realized that, in death, he had been given a gift—the chance to understand the consequences of his actions, and to see the beauty that could come from compassion and empathy.

The bear, too, found peace in knowing that her cubs were cared for, that they had found a new family who loved them as she had. She and Luke shared a moment of understanding, recognizing that, in the end, they were not so different. One had acted out of a need to protect her loved ones, and the other had learned that life was not about taking, but about giving.

The Reaper, his task complete, stood between them once more, his presence a calming force. "It is time," he said quietly to Luke and the bear, his voice carrying the weight of ancient wisdom. "You have both found the understanding you were meant to gain. Your cubs and your family, through this shared experience, discovered a different kind of love. One that brought healing, comfort, and a deeper connection. Their lives, now enriched with empathy and compassion, helped fill the void that remained from your loss. It is time to move on."

With those words, the Reaper raised his scythe, and the world around them began to fade. Luke and the bear felt themselves being lifted, their souls leaving the earthly plane and moving toward a place of peace and light. They knew that, even in death, they had found a way to coexist, to understand each other, and to leave behind a legacy of love and compassion.

And so, they moved on, leaving behind the world of the living, but taking with them the lessons they had learned. The Reaper watched them go, knowing that they had found their peace, and that life would continue, as it always does, with love and understanding at its core.

Marks of the Unseen

In the face of the inevitable, courage and justice leave a lasting mark on the world.

The Witnesses

Edmond's ankles clinked with each step as he shuffled down the long, dim hallway, the worn shackles binding his feet together barely allowing him to move. His hands, bound in front of him, rested awkwardly against the faded orange fabric of his prison jumpsuit. The slippers on his feet, once white but now stained with the grime of countless walks across the prison floors, scraped against the cold concrete with every step. His breath was steady, his eyes forward, and his lips curled into the slightest smirk. Edmond had no regrets. He felt only pride for what he had done.

The hallway seemed endless, the walls closing in on him with every step. The flickering fluorescent lights overhead cast long shadows, making the already narrow space feel even tighter. The scent of bleach and sweat filled the air, a sharp contrast to the musty, damp smell that clung to the aging bricks. Edmond barely noticed. His mind was elsewhere—on the faces of the women he had killed, the terror in their eyes, the final gasps of breath as he ended their lives. He relished those memories, savored them as he walked toward the room where his life would end.

As he reached the heavy steel door at the end of the hallway, it creaked open, revealing a small chamber. The walls were bare, painted a sickly, peeling green. The only furniture in the room was a wooden chair, old and splintered, with leather straps attached to its arms and legs. The chair's surface was worn, the wood darkened by the sweat and fear of those who had sat there before. A small bucket of water sat on the floor beside it, a sponge resting on the rim, damp and ready to serve its purpose.

Edmond hesitated for the first time, his eyes catching on the grim figure standing in the corner of the room with him. Cloaked in shadows, the Grim Reaper watched silently, a towering presence with a skeletal hand resting on the hilt of his scythe. Edmond felt a chill run down his spine but quickly pushed it aside. Fear was for the weak, and he refused to show it now, not even to himself.

The prison guards, their faces stern and impassive, motioned for Edmond to sit in the chair. He looked around the room, his gaze shifting to the observation window, a pane of thick, reinforced glass separating him from those who had come to watch him die. The lighting in the witness room was dim, but as his eyes adjusted, Edmond saw the faces of the people sitting there—twenty seats filled with individuals he didn't recognize. He knew who they were, though. These were the parents of his victims, the ones who had suffered the loss of their daughters at his hands.

As Edmond sat down in the chair, its hard surface pressing uncomfortably into his back, the lights in the observation room brightened. That's when he saw them—the souls of the women he had killed, standing behind their parents, their spectral hands resting gently on their shoulders. They were silent, their faces pale and ethereal, but their eyes burned with the memory of their deaths. The ninth victim, the one who had escaped and brought him to justice, sat with her parents in the front row, her gaze fixed on Edmond, her expression unreadable.

Edmond's smirk faded as he felt the straps tighten around his wrists and ankles, securing him to the chair. He stared at the souls of the women, his confidence slipping as their presence weighed heavily on him. Still, there was no regret—only a growing sense of fear, a fear he tried to bury as the guards prepared him for death.

The parents of the victims watched in silence, their emotions a complex mix of sorrow, anger, and a desperate need for closure. They had come to this room seeking peace, justice, and an end to the nightmares that had haunted them since the day their daughters were taken from them. For them, watching Edmond die would be the final chapter in a story that had been filled with horror and loss. It would not bring their loved ones back, but it would close a door that had been left agonizingly open for far too long.

"Any last words?" a voice asked from behind him. What could he say to those who had come to see him die? Edmond clenched his jaw, the fear now bubbling just beneath the surface.

"No," he replied, his voice steady, stripped of the bravado he once bore.

One of the guards approached Edmond with the sponge, dipping it into the bucket of water before placing it on his head, the cold water chilling his scalp. The guard then secured a leather strap over the sponge, pressing it firmly against Edmond's skull. A black hood was pulled over his face, plunging him into darkness, but even with his vision obscured, Edmond could still see the souls of his victims, their eyes locked on him as if they could see through the fabric.

The guard stepped back, and a moment later, the switch was thrown. Electricity surged through Edmond's body, his muscles tensing and convulsing as the current tore through him. The pain was excruciating, far beyond anything he had ever felt, but it wasn't just the electric current causing his agony. He was overwhelmed by a deeper, more insidious pain—the collective torment he had inflicted on his victims and their families. It was as if every moment of suffering he had caused was being visited upon him at once. Worse than the physical agony was the sight of the souls watching him, their faces calm and resolute as they witnessed his suffering. He could feel their presence, a crushing weight that bore down on him as he thrashed in the chair, the leather straps digging into his skin.

For the parents, it was a moment of grim satisfaction—a man who had caused them immeasurable pain was finally paying for his crimes. They watched with cold eyes as the life drained from Edmond's body, their hands gripping the arms of their chairs, some weeping silently, others staring with a hardened resolve. They had waited for this day, and now that it had come, they felt a release—a loosening of the knot of grief that had bound them since the moment they learned their daughters were gone.

As the electricity stopped and Edmond's body slumped in the chair, the room was silent. The Reaper stepped forward, his presence looming over the now lifeless form of the man who had taken so much from so many. Edmond's soul, still tethered to the body, lingered, confused and disoriented.

The Grim Reaper spoke, his voice a low, resonant whisper that seemed to echo within Edmond's very being. "You robbed them of their lives, Edmond. Now, you are paying for what you've done. Prepare yourself, it will be a long journey."

The souls of the victims began to fade, their duty fulfilled, their vengeance satisfied. As they departed, Edmond felt the weight of their judgment, a crushing force that dragged him down, down into the abyss where his sins awaited him. The Reaper, cold and impartial, guided him, ensuring that his soul found the place it belonged—a place where the darkness he had spread would consume him for all eternity.

As the last of the souls vanished, the parents in the observation room felt a collective release, a sigh of relief as the nightmare that had haunted them was finally over. They knew their daughters were at peace now, free from the man who had taken everything from them. And as they left the prison, they did so with the knowledge that Edmond would no longer be a part of their world, his darkness extinguished at last.

The Reaper lingered for a moment, his gaze sweeping over the now-empty chair. He did not judge the souls he harvested, but it never weighed on him to guide those like Edmond to their much-deserved fate. Justice had been served. With a final, silent nod, he turned and faded into the shadows, his task complete.

The Last Witness

MABLE WAS WALKING BACK to her dorm after an evening class, the quiet streets of her college town almost empty. The cool night air brushed against her skin, and the soft rustle of leaves in the trees was the only sound as she made her way down the dimly lit sidewalk. She was cautious, always aware of her surroundings, but she never expected the danger that lay ahead in this familiar place.

As she neared the corner of a street, a man approached her, looking lost. He was dressed in a repairman's uniform, complete with a cap that obscured most of his face. He had a business-like demeanor, the kind that didn't raise alarms. He asked her for directions, his tone polite, almost pleading. Mable hesitated, her instincts urging her to keep walking, but he seemed harmless enough—just a man needing help.

She took a step closer to point him in the right direction when, in a flash, he lunged at her. His hand, covered in a cloth, pressed firmly against her nose and mouth. A sickly-sweet odor filled her nostrils—the smell of chloroform. Panic surged through her, but the darkness came quickly, swallowing her consciousness before she could even struggle. Mable's world faded into blackness.

When she awoke, she was in the back of a van, the cold metal floor pressing against her cheek. Her mouth was gagged, and her hands and feet bound. The van rumbled beneath her, the sound of tires crunching on the road filling her ears. She blinked rapidly, trying through her panic to piece together what had happened, how long she had been out. She remembered the man, his uniform, the cloth—she knew this wasn't going to end well.

The van finally came to a stop, and she heard the door open. Heavy footsteps crunched on the gravel outside before the doors at the back of the van were thrown open. Light flooded in, momentarily blinding her. The man was there, his expression cold, lacking any emotion. He hoisted her up like she weighed nothing, slinging her over his shoulder, her head hanging down his back.

As they exited the van, Mable's world turned disorienting. She stared at the ground behind him, the crunch of gravel bouncing in her ears with every jarring step. Trying to orient herself, she craned her neck to peer around his side, catching glimpses of the house ahead. The view was upside down, adding to her confusion and dread. It was an old, dilapidated structure, almost consumed by the overgrown foliage around it. It looked like a place where nightmares lived—its windows dark, its paint peeling, its roof sagging.

Her perspective bobbed with his heavy steps, making the scene before her even more surreal. Then she noticed them—mounds of dirt scattered across the yard, uneven patches where grass had begun to grow over. Graves, she realized with a cold dread. Those were graves.

Inside, the house was even worse. The air was thick with the smell of mold and decay, and the wooden floors creaked under the man's weight. The furniture was old, covered in dust and grime, the curtains were tattered, blocking out the moonlight. He pushed open a door, its hinges groaning in protest, revealing a steep staircase leading down into darkness. The basement.

He carried her down the stairs, each step resonating through the concrete walls. The basement was like a dungeon—cold, damp, and without light except for a single, flickering bulb hanging from the ceiling. The room was barren except for a stained mattress on the floor, a rusted sink, and a bucket in the corner. Pipes ran along the ceiling, dripping water that pooled in small, grimy puddles on the floor. The walls were concrete, rough and cracked, with strange markings and scratches etched into them. She could see where others had walked before her, the floor worn in places, the air thick with despair.

He dropped her onto the mattress and left her there, tied up and helpless.

After that night, days and weeks blurred together. The man didn't speak much, only coming down to bring her food or water or to torment her in ways that left her bruised and broken, but he kept her alive. She lost track of time, her mind a fog of pain and fear. She knew there was no escape, no hope. She was just waiting for the inevitable end.

One day, the routine changed. Mable heard the front door open above, and a new set of muffled grunts. Mable's heart pounded as the basement door creaked open, and she heard the familiar footsteps descending the stairs. The man appeared, carrying another woman over his shoulder, bound, gagged, and blindfolded. He didn't say a word as he put her down on the cold floor and tied her to a beam near the pipes, securing her so she could not get away.

Mable watched in silence, her fear escalating. When he finished restraining the new victim, he instructed them both to stay quiet before he walked back up the stairs. The door slammed shut behind him.

Mable listened to the sound of his footsteps above, moving across the floor, and then silence. She didn't know what he was doing, but she feared the worst. She knew her time was running out.

In the oppressive silence, Mable whispered to the other woman. She told her everything she knew—about the man, the house, the graves outside. She gave her name, her parents' names, and every detail she could think of. She told her to be brave, to find a way to escape and bring this monster to justice. Mable knew she wasn't getting out of this, but maybe, just maybe, the other woman could.

The sound of footsteps echoed from above again. They grew louder, closer, until the basement door creaked open. The man descended the stairs, his expression cold and empty as always. He walked over to Mable, his presence hovering over her.

"Stand up," he ordered. Mable obeyed, her body trembling. He tied her hands behind her back and led her up the stairs, her heart pounding in her chest. She knew this was the end.

The cold night air hit her face as they stepped outside. The world was eerily quiet, the only sound the crunch of gravel underfoot as he led her across the yard. As they walked past the graves she'd seen weeks before, she saw a shallow pit dug into the earth ahead of her.

Before she could even process what was happening, a sharp pain exploded in her head. The blow from the shovel knocked her into the grave, her body hitting the cold earth below. The world spun as she lay there, the darkness closing in.

The man jumped into the grave with her. She felt his hands around her neck, his grip tightening as he squeezed the life out of her. She looked into his eyes—those cold, empty eyes—as he robbed her of her breath. The world faded away, taking the pain with it.

Mable lay there lifeless, her eyes open, staring into the night. The sky, once dark, gradually brightened, and the pain that had gripped her was gone. A dark figure stood over her, not the man, but someone else. He was tall, his face hidden beneath a hood, a scythe in one hand as he extended the other to Mable.

Mable took his hand and stood up. Together, they watched as the man checked her lifeless body, ensuring there was no pulse before climbing out of the grave. The Reaper's voice was soft, almost soothing.

"The world is full of darkness and evil," he said, "but justice will come to those who bring pain to others. He will pay for what he has done, just as those before him have paid."

As the Reaper spoke, the light around them dimmed, and Mable saw them—seven other women, the souls of the victims who had suffered at the hands of this man. They stood with her now, their presence a comfort in the cold night.

The Reaper explained that, when the time came, they would be there to witness his end, and the killer would feel all the pain he had inflicted on them and their families. It would not be revenge, but justice, a final act to bring peace to their souls and their loved ones.

With a gentle sweep of his arm, the years slipped by like seconds, and they found themselves in the witness room, staring through the observation window, where the man would meet his end. Mable and the other women stood behind their parents, their hands resting on their shoulders, offering comfort as they watched the man being strapped into the chair.

The man's smirk was gone, his confidence shattered as he looked into the faces of the women he had killed. The Reaper stood nearby, his eyes locked on the man, ready to guide his soul to a place where he would suffer for all eternity.

When the switch was thrown, the man's body convulsed violently. The souls of the murdered women could sense the electricity ripping through his veins like fire. But the agony of the electric chair was only a fraction of what he felt. As the current surged, a wave of unbearable torment crashed over him—each jolt carried with it the fear, the suffering, the utter hopelessness of every victim he had ever tormented. It wasn't just their pain he felt; he was also crushed by the sorrow and grief he had caused their families, the parents' anguish, the siblings' despair, the broken lives left in his wake. The Reaper had granted them the power to make him experience every scream, every tear, every desperate plea for mercy that had fallen on his deaf ears. He could feel the weight of their collective anguish crushing him, suffocating him with the terror and despair he had sown. The horror he had once inflicted now turned inward, devouring him from the inside out.

As the man's life drained away, Mable felt a sense of peace, knowing that justice had finally been served. The Reaper stepped forward, guiding the man's soul away from the world, away from the light, and into the darkness where he belonged.

Fading Light

Life, no matter how brief, deserves to be honored and remembered for the beauty it brings to the world.

The Day the Sky Fell

MILLIE, A YOUNG TRICERATOPS, was grazing with her herd in a lush valley surrounded by towering ferns and cycads. The air was warm, thick with the scent of damp earth and flowers. Millie loved the valley—it was her world, a haven where she could play with her friends and feel safe under the watchful eyes of her parents. The morning had started like any other, but by midday, a sense of unease rippled through the herd.

The sky had begun to change. It turned a fiery orange, streaked with trails of light that grew brighter and larger with every passing moment. Millie tilted her head, her frill shimmering in the strange light, and nudged her mother. "What is that?" she asked, her voice trembling.

Her mother, a strong and imposing Triceratops, lowered her head and nudged Millie closer to her father. The herd bellowed in alarm, their deep cries echoing through the valley as the ground trembled beneath their feet. Something was coming—something immense. The air grew hotter, and the strange streaks in the sky multiplied, leaving fiery trails behind them.

The first impacts came with deafening explosions. Trees shattered into splinters, and the earth heaved violently. Millie stumbled, her small legs struggling to keep her upright as her parents flanked her, their horns raised defensively. The herd was scattering, some fleeing toward the hills while others froze in panic.

The sky erupted in blinding light as the asteroid struck. The sound was indescribable—a roar that seemed to split the world apart. Millie felt the heat before she saw the wall of fire racing toward them. Her parents roared, trying to shield her, but there was no escape. The world was unraveling.

Amidst the destruction, the Grim Reaper stood silently on a ridge overlooking the valley. His black robe flowed like shadows through the fiery winds, his scythe reflecting the chaos in its cold, sharp blade. He paused to take in the world ablaze—the trees turning to ash, rivers boiling away, and countless lives fading in an instant. The weight of the souls he had already collected pressed heavily upon him, but his duty was far from over. The end of this era marked another chapter in the endless cycle of life and death.

He had seen countless species rise and fall, each one leaving its mark upon the earth before fading into history. The earth would recover, as it always had, and life would once more find a way to flourish. There would be an age where he collected fewer souls, but his task would never truly end. Life was persistent, and so too was its inevitable end. In moments like these, he had to reconcile his eternal duty with the sorrow of witnessing such loss.

As the searing heat engulfed her, Millie felt a strange calm descend. The flames froze, the noise faded, and the chaos stilled. Before her stood a dark figure cloaked in black, his robe billowing like smoke in the fiery wind. In his bony hand, he held a scythe that gleamed with otherworldly light. His face, hidden beneath his hood, seemed to radiate an ancient sadness.

"Millie," the Grim Reaper's voice was deep and resonant, carrying both sorrow and comfort. "The earth has endured a great catastrophe—a massive asteroid has struck. You and your kind will not survive this."

"Where are my parents?" Millie asked, her voice barely a whisper.

"They are here," he said, stepping aside. Her parents stood behind him, their forms radiant and whole, free from the burns and terror of the mortal world.

The Reaper knelt before Millie, his hollow eyes meeting hers. "Come with me. I will take you to a place where there is no pain, no destruction. Only peace."

Millie's fear melted as she stepped toward her parents. They nuzzled her gently, their warmth filling her soul. Together, they followed the Reaper, leaving the shattered world behind for a realm of endless green and unbroken skies.

As he led them away, the Reaper turned back for one final glance at the dying world. He took no pleasure in this, but neither did he despair. He existed to bear witness to the ends and beginnings of all things. This was not the first time, and it would not be the last. Resolute, he tightened his grip on the scythe and disappeared into the stillness beyond the flames.

The Last Breath

MAE, A TOWERING BRACHIOSAURUS, stood near a drying riverbed, her long neck stretched toward the horizon. The forest around her, once vibrant with life, was dying. Ash coated the trees, and the air was thick with sulfur. Mae had spent her days wandering with her small group, searching for the dwindling vegetation that remained. Her massive size made her resilient, but even she felt the toll of the relentless hunger and poisoned air.

She had survived the impact weeks ago, though it had shattered the sky and set the world aflame. The sun was now a faint glow behind a veil of ash, and the days were unnaturally cold. Volcanic eruptions had darkened the sky, spewing rivers of lava that carved through the land. Mae had seen others fall—her companions, her offspring—all claimed by the unrelenting destruction.

Now, she could barely stand. Each breath was a struggle, and her once-proud form swayed with exhaustion. As she lowered her massive head to the ground, she noticed a shadow falling over her. Not from the choking ash, but from something else. Something ... otherworldly.

A figure emerged from the haze, tall and cloaked in flowing black. His scythe reflected the dim, fiery glow of the lava rivers. The Grim Reaper moved with a solemn grace, his presence both fearsome and strangely comforting. He paused before Mae, gazing at her with eyes that seemed to hold the weight of every soul he had ever taken.

"Is it my time?" Mae rasped, her deep voice heavy with sorrow.

"Yes," the Reaper replied, his voice as soft as the dying wind. "Your world is ending. It will take millions of years for the earth to heal from this. Your kind will not see it."

Mae's eyes, dull with pain, looked toward the horizon. "End my suffering," she pleaded. "And theirs."

"I cannot alter what is already unfolding," the Reaper said gently. "But I can stay with you until it is time. I can ease the pain."

Mae felt a warmth spread through her as the Reaper placed his skeletal hand on her massive shoulder. The ache in her body dulled, and the crushing sorrow lifted. Around her, the dying cries of other dinosaurs softened, as if the Reaper's presence extended to them as well.

"This is not the end," the Reaper said, his voice carrying a quiet power. "Your kind will live on in another existence, free from the destruction of this world."

As Mae took her final breath, the Reaper raised his scythe, and a soft glow enveloped her. She felt light, unburdened, and as her soul separated from her body, she saw others waiting for her. They stood in a verdant land, untouched by fire or ash, their forms strong and whole once more.

The Reaper guided Mae to join them, his dark figure a steady presence amidst the endless renewal of life. Together, they left the broken earth, their spirits soaring into a realm where no shadow could touch them.

Unyielding Spirits

Real strength is found in the choices we make for others, even when they come at a cost.

The Fight Against the Darkness

ANNIE WAS ONLY SEVEN when a terrible accident changed her life forever. It happened so fast—a car crash that left her in a hospital bed, trapped in a coma. She lay motionless, fighting for her life. Days turned to weeks, weeks turned to months, all the while, little Annie was caught in the delicate space between life and death.

Her parents stayed by her side day and night, whispering words of love and encouragement, hoping their presence would somehow reach her. The steady beep of machines and the sterile smell of the hospital filled the room.

Annie's body was struggling to heal from the injuries that had overtaken it. Her spirit, however, was not alone in this battle. One evening, when the hospital was quiet and time seemed to stand still, the Grim Reaper appeared at Annie's bedside. His cloak of shadows seemed almost comforting as he stood there, watching her with empathy and understanding of the battle she faced.

"You're in a place between," he said gently. "Annie, the struggle for life is a fight worth having. You have a strength inside you that can get you through this. Fight, Annie. Push back against the darkness. Fight to live, and you'll become someone who can handle anything."

Though Annie wouldn't remember this encounter, the Reaper's message lingered deep within her. His words planted a seed of resolve that would grow over time and get her through the hardest times. For now, his work was done. He vanished, knowing he would one day see Annie again, but not for a while.

Over the next days, Annie began showing signs of improvement. She was fighting for her life. When Annie finally woke up, everything was different. Her parents cried tears of relief and hugged her tightly, their hearts full of gratitude and love. But Annie looked at them with eyes that didn't recognize their faces. It was like she had stepped into a world where nothing felt familiar.

She had forgotten everything—her memories were gone, and her body felt weak and unsteady. Annie had to relearn everything she had already known. The simple things most people take for granted, like walking and talking, were now daunting tasks. Her legs were weak, her steps unsure, and her mind felt empty.

Her memories of the past had vanished, leaving a blank slate. Though some memories would eventually return, it would take months, even years, for them to come back, and many would never be recovered. It was as if her life's story had been erased, and she had to write it all over again.

Annie, young as she was, found a spark of determination inside her. She wanted to remember, and to become strong again. Annie embraced the challenges, driven by the belief that one day, she would reclaim her life.

The accident had taken much from her, but it had also ignited something deep within—a quiet determination to take back her life. Her journey to recovery was long and challenging. Annie had to learn everything anew. Her body, once full of energy, now moved with uncertainty and caution. Yet, her spirit shone brightly, and she was filled with a new sense of purpose. Her laughter filled the hospital with life, reminding everyone of her strength.

Annie grew into a confident young woman, and though she bore the scars of her battle, she wore them with pride. They were not marks of weakness but of someone who had survived and emerged stronger.

Annie grew up surrounded by family who cherished every moment with her. Her parents, who had been there from the start, saw her determination firsthand and were inspired by her strength.

Annie became a wife and a mother, then a grandmother, and her story of strength became an inspiration for her children and grandchildren. She taught them to fight for what they believed in and never to give up.

Annie lived a good life. She dedicated herself to helping others, always showing compassion and care. Her heart was vast, and her love for others knew no bounds.

Decades later, Annie found herself at another crossroads. A severe illness had taken hold, threatening to extinguish the light she had fought so hard to keep alive. She sat in her beautiful home overlooking the ocean, a place of peace and reflection. The rhythmic sound of waves crashing against the shore was a soothing lullaby, comforting her weary spirit.

It was there, surrounded by memories of a life well lived, that the Grim Reaper returned. He appeared before her, a familiar presence that sparked a sudden recognition. Annie, though tired from the battle she now faced, felt a sense of calm in his presence.

"You've come a long way, Annie," the Reaper said, his voice carrying a note of admiration. "I'm proud of you. You've fought hard and turned challenges into triumphs. I've watched you grow and become someone who inspires everyone around you."

Annie looked at him, her eyes filled with understanding. She remembered the feeling from long ago, that gentle push that had set her on the path to becoming who she was meant to be.

"You no longer have to fight," the Reaper assured her. "You've lived a full life, leaving behind a legacy of strength and love. It's time to rest."

Annie nodded, a smile on her lips as she closed her eyes for the last time. She knew that her journey was complete, that she had done all she could in this life.

As the Grim Reaper gently took Annie's soul, he marveled at the legacy she left behind—a story of courage and compassion. She had shown the world what it meant to be a fighter, inspiring generations to come.

In the hearts of her family, Annie's spirit would live on, a light in times of darkness. Her story, one of perseverance, would be told for years to come.

The Reunion

CHARLIE WAS NAMED AFTER his father, Charles, making him the second in his family to bear the name, officially known as Charles II. However, everyone simply called him Charlie, just like his dad. As the cherished only child in a small, close-knit family, Charlie thrived on the love and attention of his parents. In the quiet town they called home, life moved at a gentle pace, a welcome contrast to the rush and chaos of city life. This slower, more intimate way of living was something Charlie and his parents cherished deeply.

Charlie's father was a truck driver, navigating the vast highways that crisscrossed state lines, transporting cargo from one corner of the country to another. It was a demanding job, filled with long hours and the constant awareness that any mistake could be catastrophic. But Charlie's father was meticulous, always cautious, always alert. He knew that his safe return home was everything to his wife and son.

Charlie idolized his father, hanging on every word of the stories he would tell about his travels—tales of endless roads, towering mountains, and open skies. Every morning his father left for a long haul, Charlie would shuffle out of bed, following him from room to room, begging to join him on his journeys. Charlie always knew what the answer would be, but figured he would ask anyway. Although he couldn't go, his father's vivid storytelling made Charlie feel as if he were right there, sitting in the passenger seat beside him, experiencing every sight and sound of the road.

One day, their world was shattered by an unexpected blow. Charlie fell ill—an illness that began with mild symptoms but quickly escalated into something far more severe. Despite the doctors' best efforts, the diagnosis was terminal. Even as his condition worsened, Charlie continued to ask his father if he could accompany him on his trips, dreaming of the day he might finally get to see the world outside his small town. But his father knew that day would never come. He kept the stories alive, adding even more detailed tales, knowing in his heart that Charlie would never experience those places himself.

Charlie's father took on extra work, driving longer routes to pay the mounting medical bills. It broke his heart to be away from his ailing son, but he did what he had to do for his family. Meanwhile, Charlie's mother stayed by his side, her heart aching with every moment she watched her son weaken.

One early morning, when the moon hung low in the sky, Charlie's father prepared for yet another long journey. He went through his routine, but something was different. The house was eerily quiet. Charlie, who usually dragged himself out of bed to see his father off, didn't appear. Concerned, his father climbed the stairs to Charlie's room.

There, he found his son lying weakly in bed, too frail to move. The father sat beside him, gently pulling him into a hug. "I love you, boy," he whispered, trying to hold back the tears.

Charlie, sensing his father's worry, reassured him with a faint smile. "I'll be okay, Dad. I can't wait to hear all about your trip when you get back." He hugged his father a little longer than usual, clinging to the warmth of his embrace. As his father walked out the door, Charlie whispered, "I love you, Dad," knowing deep down that this might be the last time.

With a heavy heart, Charlie's father left for work. Every mile on the road felt longer than usual. He couldn't stop thinking about his son, so at every opportunity, he called home to check on him. Each time, his wife's voice was filled with the same sadness, but there was no new news. Charlie was holding on, but just barely.

Then, as he approached the border of another state, his phone rang. His wife was on the other end, her voice choked with tears.

"He's gone," she sobbed. "Our boy is gone."

The news hit him like a ton of bricks. He pulled his truck over to the side of the road, unable to drive through the flood of emotions. Tears streamed down his face as he listened to his wife's sobs, feeling utterly helpless. The worst had happened, and he hadn't been there to say goodbye.

They laid Charlie to rest in a small, peaceful cemetery. The funeral was quiet, attended only by close family. The pain of losing his only son was unbearable, but after everyone left, Charlie's father stayed behind. He sat beside Charlie's grave, telling him all about his trip, just as he would have if Charlie had been waiting for him at home. It was his way of saying goodbye, of making it home to his son.

Returning to the routine, he felt Charlie's absence in every corner of the house. Still, each morning before he left, he would go upstairs, sit on the bed where Charlie had spent his final months, and talk to him as if he were still there. When he returned from work trips, he would do the same, recounting every detail of the journey, just as he had always done. In those moments, he could almost feel Charlie's presence, as if his son were listening, smiling at the stories he loved so much.

On the long drives, he began to pretend that Charlie was with him, sitting in the passenger seat, just as he had always wished. He spoke aloud, recounting the sights and sounds of the road, and it brought him comfort. He could feel Charlie's presence, especially when fatigue set in, and the road grew long. It was as if Charlie were there, nudging him awake, keeping him safe.

Years passed, but the pain of losing Charlie never truly faded. On what would have been Charlie's birthdays, his father would talk to him as though he were still growing up, imagining the advice he'd give and the milestones they would celebrate together. It was his way of keeping Charlie alive, even in memory.

Then, one day, everything changed.

Charlie's father was driving his truck on a familiar route when disaster struck. A sudden accident left him critically injured. As paramedics worked to save him, he found himself drifting between life and death. In that hazy space, he saw a dark figure standing before him—a tall, hooded figure holding a scythe. The Reaper's presence was ominous, his dark robe flowing like shadows, his scythe gleaming with a cold, metallic edge.

But there was someone else there too. A young man, strong and healthy, with a face full of love. It was Charlie, no longer the sickly child he remembered but a vibrant, healthy young man. Despite the years that had passed, the father recognized his son instantly, his heart swelling with emotion.

"Father," Charlie said softly, his voice filled with warmth. "It's not your time yet. You have to pull through. I'm still here with you, and I always will be."

Charlie's father's heart swelled with emotion. He had always felt Charlie's presence, but seeing him now, standing strong and whole, filled him with a deep sense of peace.

"I never got to say goodbye," Charlie continued, "but I never left your side. I've been with you on every journey, just as you always imagined. Thank you for keeping me alive in your thoughts."

Tears filled the father's eyes as he reached out to his son. "Are you okay, son?" he whispered.

"I'm more than okay," Charlie replied, his smile gentle and reassuring. "There's no more pain, no more suffering. I've been with you through every story you've shared, every conversation you've had with me, I was there. I've traveled every mile alongside you, experiencing all the things I ever dreamed of—most of all, I cherished every moment spent with you. I've never left your side. I just wanted to finally tell you, to hug you, and to let you know that I'll always be here, with you."

Charlie stepped forward, wrapping his arms around his father. It was a moment of pure, unconditional love. The embrace felt real, as though they were both alive, holding each other in a world that transcended life and death. They held on for a long time, neither wanting to let go, both savoring the connection they had missed for so long.

"I love you, Dad," Charlie said softly. "And I'll always be by your side. But you have to keep going. Mom needs you."

His father nodded, his heart full of love and sorrow. "I'll keep going, son. For you, and for her."

The Grim Reaper, standing silently in the background, never uttered a word. He understood the bond between father and son and allowed them this moment of connection. They all had an unspoken understanding of his role, and it was through the Reaper's presence that Charlie was able to stay in this realm, to take care of his father and let him know they would see each other again.

As Charlie and the Reaper began to fade, Charlie's father felt a deep sense of peace. He had been given a gift—a chance to see his son, to know that he was okay, and to say goodbye.

The paramedics managed to revive him, and he survived the accident. As he lay in the hospital recovering, he knew that Charlie was still with him. The encounter had brought him a peace he hadn't felt in years, knowing that one day, when the Reaper returned, he would be reunited with his son.

Until then, he would live his life in a way that honored the memory of the boy he loved so dearly.

The Choice

Henry lay motionless on the cold concrete, the sounds around him muffled and distant. His body was broken, twisted at unnatural angles, and pain shot through him with every shallow breath. He could barely keep his eyes open, but when he did, he caught glimpses of the chaos around him—fellow workers shouting, their voices distant, muffled, like they were underwater, the screeching of cranes coming to a halt, and the blaring of sirens in the distance.

The air was filled with dust and the metallic scent of blood—his blood. He tried to move, to lift his arm, but his body refused to obey. His thoughts were a jumble of confusion and pain, but one thing was clear: he was badly hurt, possibly dying.

The wind whipped through the open construction site, and as he lay there, his mind began to drift. He thought of his wife, of his two sons, and the life they had built together. They had always worried about him working at such heights, but he had reassured them time and time again that he was careful, that he knew what he was doing. Now, he wasn't so sure.

Henry was no stranger to the dangers of his job. As a builder working on high-rise buildings, he knew that every day came with risks. But he had never imagined that one of those risks would change his life—or end it.

The morning of the accident, Henry was up on the thirtieth floor of the building, securing steel beams. The wind was strong, but he was used to that. His hands were steady, his mind focused on the task at hand. Suddenly, something went wrong. The crane operator above him miscalculated the swing of a massive steel beam, and before Henry could react, the beam came crashing down, clipping the scaffolding where he stood.

Time seemed to slow as Henry felt the impact. The scaffolding beneath him gave way, and he was thrown off balance. He reached out, grabbing for anything to stop his fall, but his hands found only air. He remembered the sudden lurch, the feeling of weightlessness as he fell, the sickening crunch as he hit the ground below. The pain had been instant, searing through his body like wildfire. Now, as he lay there, he felt his life slipping away, his vision darkening around the edges.

The next few moments were a blur of pain and confusion. The paramedics arrived, their voices urgent as they assessed the situation. Henry could barely hear them over the roar in his ears, but he knew they were trying to save him. They lifted him onto a stretcher, the world spinning as they moved. He tried to focus, to hold on, but it was so hard. His vision dimmed as he lay there, surrounded by pain. It was too much. Everything went black.

When he came to, he was in the back of an ambulance, the sirens wailing as they sped through the streets. The paramedics were working frantically, their faces tense with concentration. They didn't give up. Henry could feel his life slipping away, the edges of his vision darkening once more. He knew he was in bad shape—he could feel it in the way his body refused to respond, in the numbness that was creeping over him. Henry thought of his family waiting for him at home as he began to fade.

As Henry hovered on the brink of consciousness, something strange happened. He became aware of another presence in the ambulance. It was a figure cloaked in darkness, its face hidden beneath a hood, holding a scythe in its skeletal hand. Henry should have been terrified, but instead, he felt a strange sense of calm. The Reaper stood silently beside him, watching as the paramedics worked to save his life.

"You know why I'm here, Henry," the Reaper said, his voice low and resonant, echoing within Henry's mind rather than through the air.

Henry swallowed hard, the weight of the situation pressing down on him. "Am I ... am I going to die?"

"No Henry, you are not going to die," the Reaper replied, stepping closer, the scythe gleaming ominously in the dim light of the ambulance. The Reaper tilted his head slightly. "You have a choice to make. You will survive this accident, but it will come at a high cost, not only to you and your family but to the lives of others. Those who desperately need what you can give—will perish."

Henry's brow furrowed in confusion. "What do you mean?" His heart pounded in his chest, not from fear, but from the weight of the decision placed before him. "Who?" he managed to ask. "Who would die if I live?"

The Reaper extended a hand, and suddenly, the scene around them shifted. They were no longer in the ambulance. Instead, they stood in a small, sterile hospital room. Henry looked around, bewildered, and then his gaze fell on the figure lying in the bed.

A teenage boy, not older than fifteen, clung to life by a thread. His body was frail and weak, hooked up to machines that beeped rhythmically in the silence. His skin pale, his eyes sunken, and his family gathered around him, their faces etched with despair, knowing that their time with him was running out.

"This boy," the Reaper said softly, "needs a kidney. One of yours could save his life, but if you survive, he will die waiting for a donor."

Henry felt a lump in his throat as he watched the boy's mother clutching his hand, her red-rimmed eyes betraying hours of crying. The boy's father stood by the window, staring out blankly, his shoulders heavy with despair. Henry could feel their helplessness, their grief, and it cut through him.

"It's not just him," the Reaper continued, and with a wave of his hand, they were in another room, another hospital. A middle-aged woman lay in a bed, her eyes closed, her breathing labored. Her family was there too, whispering prayers and holding onto fading hope.

"This woman," the Reaper said, "is on the verge of death. She needs a liver transplant, and soon. Without it, she will not survive the night."

Henry's chest tightened as he looked at the woman and her family. He thought of his own wife and two sons, imagining them in this situation. The woman's mother was holding her hand, tears streaming down her face, while her father stood nearby, his expression one of silent defeat.

"And it's not just the boy and the woman," the Reaper said, his voice solemn. Another wave of his hand brought them to more hospital rooms. Henry saw patients of all ages, waiting for kidneys, lungs, and other vital organs. A young man sat weakly beside his fiancée, her hands trembling as she held his. An elderly man lay surrounded by his grown children, each preparing to say goodbye.

Henry's emotions overwhelmed him. "Why are you showing me this?" he asked, his voice trembling. "You said I wouldn't die."

The Reaper turned toward him, his dark robe shifting like smoke. "Because you have a choice, Henry. You were meant to survive this accident. But if you do, all these people—people whose lives you could save—will die. You have the power to change their fates. You can sacrifice yourself so they can live." Henry stood silent, the weight of the decision pressing down on him.

"Henry," the Reaper said gently, "I must collect a soul tonight. Whether it's yours or theirs is up to you."

Henry felt his heart pound in his chest. The thought of dying was terrifying, but the thought of living at the cost of others' lives was unbearable. He pictured his wife, his sons. He had always been there for them, and the idea of leaving them behind was almost too much to bear.

The Reaper stood quietly, allowing Henry to process everything he had seen. Henry's thoughts turned to his own family—his wife, his two sons.

"What about my family?" Henry asked, his voice barely above a whisper. "How will they manage without me?"

The Reaper placed a skeletal hand on Henry's shoulder, a surprisingly gentle touch. "Your family will grieve, but they will also find strength in your sacrifice. Your wife will be cared for, and your sons will grow up knowing their father was a man of great courage and compassion. They will understand that you made this choice out of love—for them and for others. And you will not truly leave them. You will always be with them in spirit, guiding them, watching over them."

Henry's tears fell freely now as he thought of his sons, the way they looked up to him, the way they would carry on without him. He thought of his wife, how strong she was, how she would guide them through this. And he thought of those other families, the ones who would lose their loved ones if he chose to live. He also knew that it was a new beginning for those whose lives he would save.

Henry closed his eyes, tears streaming down his face. The decision weighed heavily on him, but in his heart, he knew what he had to do.

"I'll do it," Henry whispered. "I'll give my life for them—for the boy and the others. Tell my family that I love them, and that I'm at peace with this decision."

The Reaper nodded, a look of solemn respect in his eyes. "Your sacrifice will not be in vain, Henry. You will give others the chance to continue their lives. Your family will understand, and they will find peace."

Henry closed his eyes, his heart filled with a deep sense of fulfillment. He had done what was right, what was necessary. His life was ending, but in doing so, he was giving others a chance to live. The pain in his body began to fade, and he knew that his decision had been the right one. "Will they know?" he asked. "Will they know why I did this?"

"Yes," the Reaper said. As they mourn your loss, they will feel your presence, and they will know that you are at peace."

The Reaper raised his scythe, and as he did, Henry felt a warmth spread through him. The ambulance faded away, replaced by darkness, and then by light—a soft, comforting light. Henry knew he was passing on, but he also knew that he was leaving something behind, something that would live on in the lives of those he had saved.

Back in the operating room, Henry's body was failing. The surgeons worked desperately to save him, but they knew the outcome was inevitable. His heart was barely functioning, sustained only by the machines. His family, waiting outside, was informed of his dire condition. Amid their grief, the doctors approached them with a difficult question—a question about organ donation. And despite their sorrow, Henry's wife and sons made the decision to honor his memory by giving life to others. It was as if they knew this was Henry's last wish.

As Henry's soul stood beside the Reaper, watching his family through the window, he felt a deep sense of peace. He saw them hold each other, finding strength in their love and in knowing that he had made a difference. The Reaper turned to Henry, his hooded face softening with a touch of respect.

"You made the right choice, Henry. Your sacrifice will save many lives, and your family is proud of you. They will carry your memory with them, and they will be strong."

Henry nodded, tears of both sadness and joy in his eyes. "Thank you," he said, his voice steady. "For giving me the choice."

The Reaper placed a hand on Henry's back, guiding him toward the light. "It's time to rest now, Henry. Your journey here is over, but there is more waiting for you."

Henry looked back one last time, seeing his family standing together, united in their grief but also in their love. He knew he would see them again, and when he did, it would be as if no time had passed at all.

With a final breath, Henry stepped into the light, the Reaper by his side, and the world faded away, leaving behind only peace.

A Quiet Sacrifice

MILTON'S FARM WAS A patchwork of hard work and history, nestled in the quiet rural stretch of South Dakota that had been in his family for generations. The modest farmhouse sat surrounded by golden fields of corn and wheat that stretched to the horizon. A sturdy red barn stood nearby, sheltering an array of animals: two horses, a few dozen hens, several goats, a small herd of cattle, and a couple of stubborn pigs that always seemed to test his patience. His loyal dog was always by his side, whether herding the cattle, fetching tools, or simply keeping him company during the long days. The air smelled of fresh hay, earth, and the faint scent of the wood-burning stove from the kitchen where Milton's wife was making dinner.

Every day was a predictable rhythm. Milton rose before dawn, checked on the animals, worked the fields, and returned to his family for dinner. He loved the simplicity of his life, finding purpose in every small task. His wife often teased him about his meticulous schedules, but Milton knew that a farm thrived on routine, and he hoped one day to pass it all down to his son.

Life here was simple and quiet—until it wasn't. Tornado season brought with it a tension that never fully dissipated. The family had taken every precaution. An underground bunker sat not far from the barn, reinforced to shelter them and as many animals as possible. But Milton knew all too well that preparation could only go so far against nature's fury.

It was a morning like so many others on the farm. Milton was up before dawn, walking the perimeter of the farm with a mug of coffee in hand. His dog padded alongside him, his ears alert to every rustle in the fields. The air was heavy and still, a warning that only a farmer would notice. By afternoon, the sky began to shift. The soft blue gave way to ominous, churning clouds. A stark line divided the heavens—dark, brooding gray on top and an unnatural brightness on the bottom. The air was electric, charged with anticipation.

The local weather station confirmed his fears: severe storms were on their way, with the potential for tornadoes. Milton and his wife exchanged a knowing look. She gathered their baby girl and son, setting up supplies in the bunker while Milton turned his attention to the animals.

"We'll be fine," he reassured her, his voice steady. He kissed his wife and then bent down to hug his children tightly. His dog nudged Milton's hand, sensing the urgency in his tone. Milton scratched behind his ears and whispered, "Stay close, old boy. We've got work to do."

Milton worked methodically, moving the smaller animals into the shelter first—the hens clucked in protest as he carried them in crates, and the goats followed reluctantly, bleating their displeasure. His dog darted back and forth, herding the more stubborn animals with precision born of years of instinct and partnership. Together, they made quick work of rounding up the smaller creatures.

Knowing the storm was closing in, Milton knelt at the door of the bunker with his dog. Hugging him tightly, Milton whispered, "Watch over them, old boy." His voice was thick with emotion. The dog licked Milton's face, his tail wagging faintly despite the fear in his eyes. Milton pushed the door closed, ensuring the safety of his family and loyal companion before heading back to secure the remaining animals.

The wind began to pick up, pushing against him with every step. He secured the barn doors and turned to the larger animals. The two horses were spooked, their nostrils flaring as they stomped nervously. It took all of Milton's strength to lead them toward the shelter. The cattle were harder to manage; they sensed the coming storm and resisted his coaxing. He finally got them to safety, his shirt soaked with sweat despite the cooling wind.

Then, the sirens wailed.

The tornado was near. The horizon darkened as the massive funnel cloud tore across the fields, a roaring monster that shredded everything in its path. Debris filled the air—wood splinters, shingles, and unrecognizable scraps. Milton sprinted toward the shelter, fighting against the ferocious wind. His heart pounded as he reached for the door, but it wouldn't budge. It was locked, just as he'd secured it earlier to protect his family.

The wind grew stronger, lifting him off his feet. He clung to the door handle until his grip gave way. The world spun as the storm carried him, his body weightless in the chaos. For a brief moment, he saw the barn standing untouched, a miracle amidst the destruction. Then everything went dark.

When Milton opened his eyes, he was no longer in the storm. He stood in a field bathed in golden sunlight, the sky a perfect, cloudless blue. The air smelled sweet, like blooming flowers and fresh rain. Beside him stood the Grim Reaper, cloaked in a simple black robe, holding his scythe. His face was not menacing but kind, his eyes reflecting the depth of every soul he had guided.

"I'm here for you, Milton," the Reaper said, his voice calm and steady.

Milton didn't flinch. He felt no fear, only sadness that he wouldn't be able to hold his family again.

"Are they safe?" Milton asked.

The Reaper extended a hand, and the scenery shifted. They were now inside the bunker. Milton saw his wife holding their baby, his son clutching her arm tightly. At their feet sat his dog, eyes alert and body poised protectively, offering comfort and reassurance to the family. Around them, the animals were huddled together, safe and unharmed, as they waited for the storm above to pass.

"They are safe because of you," the Reaper said. "You gave everything for them, Milton," he added gently. "Because of your strength and sacrifice, they have a future."

Milton felt a wave of peace wash over him. He looked at his family one last time, their love filling every corner of his being.

"They'll rebuild," the Reaper assured him. "The barn was spared, and they will carry on your legacy. Your son will grow up knowing the farm you fought to protect."

As the Reaper guided him away, the storm faded. The chaos gave way to a serene sky painted with soft hues of pink and orange. A rainbow arched across the horizon, a symbol of hope and renewal. Milton felt himself dissolve into the beauty of the moment, the weight of his sacrifice lifted.

End of an Age

Each era leaves its mark, reminding us that even as times change, the essence of what once was—remains.

Wings of Valor

High atop the tallest mountain, where clouds wrapped around rugged cliffs and icy peaks, lived Valkeryth, the most majestic of dragons. He was a breathtaking sight, his scales a vibrant blend of crimson and sapphire, shimmering like polished gemstones under the sunlight. His wings stretched wide and powerful, their edges gleaming silver as they cut through the air, carrying him higher than any other dragon dared to go. His long tail, streaked with gold, curled elegantly behind him, and his horns arched backward—sharp, black as charcoal, radiating an ethereal gleam.

Valkeryth's name had been chosen with great care by his parents. On the day he hatched, his father cradled the tiny dragon in his powerful claws, gazing at him with pride. "We shall call you Valkeryth," he whispered, his voice a deep rumble filled with love, "because you will be a dragon of valor, unyielding and brave, and with the endurance to weather all storms. You will guard the skies and become a protector for our kind." From that moment, they believed he was destined for greatness. As the years passed, Valkeryth lived up to his name, becoming a symbol of courage and resilience—admired by his kin and feared by all who threatened their peace.

Valkeryth and his equally magnificent mate shared their lives atop the grandest mountain, high above the forests and rivers that sprawled far below. Other dragons found homes on distant peaks, their wings gliding with graceful precision—some feathered with blue streaks, others tipped with ebony. Together, they filled the sky with magic, soaring through endless blue, their presence a testament to the ancient power of their kind. They lived in harmony, their only unspoken rule: stay far from human lands. From ancient times to the present, dragons knew the cruelty humanity inflicted upon what it feared.

Valkeryth and his mate spent their days gliding over mountaintops, dipping through clouds, and watching the seasons change beneath them. Their joy, however, centered on something greater—two eggs they guarded with tender care. For years, they had nurtured them, waiting patiently for the day they would hatch.

One morning, as the first light of dawn swept across the mountain peaks, the eggs began to stir. Valkeryth and his mate coiled protectively around them, a gentle heat radiating from their fiery interiors and enveloping the eggs in a nurturing glow. The first egg cracked open, revealing an emerald-hued hatchling with delicate wings and bright amber eyes, its spirit already echoing its father's strength. Moments later, the second egg broke, and out emerged another—a sapphire-colored sibling with silver streaks shimmering along its scales.

The sight of their newborn dragons filled Valkeryth and his mate with overwhelming joy. They had waited so long for this moment, and now their family was complete.

Years passed, and the two young dragons grew into majestic beings. Their scales glimmered beneath the sun, and their wings grew stronger with each flight. Valkeryth and his mate nurtured them with unwavering care, guiding them through the skies and teaching them the ways of the dragons. Together, they soared over mountain ranges, glided above forests, and dipped into valleys. Valkeryth watched with pride as his sons grew into capable guardians, knowing they would carry the legacy of their kind forward.

Then came the day that changed everything. It was a morning like any other—Valkeryth and his mate flew side by side, their wings slicing through the crisp air as they soared over rivers and valleys. But as they crossed the edge of a forest, Valkeryth saw them: thousands of men, dressed in gleaming armor, marching like a dark tide across the land.

The soldiers carried weapons of war—arrows, swords, catapults—and heavy nets draped over their shoulders, glinting ominously under the sun.

"They come for us," Valkeryth rumbled, his voice deep and ominous. "We must leave. We cannot win this fight."

But it was too late. Arrows shot through the sky with deadly precision. His mate twisted mid-flight, roaring in defiance as a net ensnared her wings. Valkeryth watched in horror as she tumbled toward the earth, chains wrapping around her limbs, pulling her down. She fought against the bindings, but the soldiers swarmed her like a plague.

Fury burned in Valkeryth's chest. With a mighty roar, he unleashed a torrent of fire upon the army below, incinerating hundreds of men in his rage. His flames consumed everything—trees, wagons, and soldiers alike. But the army pressed on, driven by fear and hatred. They hurled spears and arrows, their weapons piercing his vibrant scales. Chains coiled around his wings and legs, dragging him from the sky. His body, once strong and majestic, now lay broken and bleeding under the relentless assault.

Through the smoke and chaos, Valkeryth saw his mate pinned beneath the soldiers' nets. Her golden eyes locked with his—filled with sorrow, but also acceptance. She knew their time had come.

But in their final moments, they found solace, knowing that their sons would live on—far from the cruelty of humans.

Through the smoke and ruin, the Grim Reaper glided silently across the battlefield. He moved without a sound, collecting the souls of the fallen—men, horses, and forest creatures alike—until he stood before the two dragons. Valkeryth, his breath shallow, lifted his head weakly to meet the Reaper's gaze.

"Rest now, great ones," the Reaper whispered, his voice like a calm breeze through the night. "Your time here is done, but your legacy will endure."

Valkeryth's mate closed her eyes first, the Reaper's hand resting gently upon her. With a final breath, Valkeryth followed, his spirit rising from his broken body. As their souls ascended, the Reaper offered them one last comfort.

"Your sons will carry your strength forward, and they will know peace for many years to come."

Together, Valkeryth and his mate drifted into the ephemeral world, where the other dragons awaited them—creatures of legend who had long left the mortal realm.

The Reaper lingered a moment longer, his shadowy figure watching over the battlefield. He knew that the era of dragons was drawing to a close. It was not yet time, but the end was near.

Perched atop the highest peak, Dexter and his brother gazed out over the distant landscape. The sky was heavy with smoke, and the faint glow of fires flickered far across the horizon. They could make out the restless movements below—the telltale signs of a battle unfolding—though the details were lost in the haze and distance. All they knew was that their parents were there, fighting amidst the chaos. And then, the flickers of movement stopped, vanishing into the thick curtain of smoke and fire.

The brothers stood motionless, watching as the last traces of the fight faded into the horizon. Though they couldn't see what had happened, they knew deep in their hearts that their parents would not be returning.

The Grim Reaper passed through in silence, his presence unseen but undeniable. Like a breeze brushing through the clouds or the faintest shift in the wind, his essence lingered, filling the young dragons with a strange and bittersweet calm. Though their hearts ached, they knew—without needing to speak—that they were alone now. And with that knowledge came clarity: they would carry on, as their parents had prepared them to, guarding the skies and their kind, honoring the legacy left behind.

The Reaper stood at the edge of the mountain, watching the young dragons disappear into the clouds. He knew their time on Earth would be long, but even they could not escape the fate that awaited all creatures.

Yet, in the ephemeral world, Valkeryth and his mate soared freely across endless skies, waiting for the day their sons would join them—far from the reach of human hands, their spirits unbroken.

The Reaper blended into the mist, leaving the waterfall, the mountains, and the memories of the dragons to rest in peace.

Voices of the Wild

The natural world holds beauty and lessons, reminding us to cherish all life with compassion.

Keeper of Hearts

Timmy was just nine years old, a bright-eyed boy with tousled brown hair that often fell into his eyes, and a smile that could light up a room. His parents were hardworking and loved him dearly, but their busy schedules made them believe they couldn't care for a pet. So, Timmy found another way to fill the void left by the absence of a furry friend.

Timmy's heart belonged to animals, especially those without homes. He was drawn to the creatures that others overlooked. Every day after school, he would rush to the local animal shelter, spending hours petting the dogs, playing with the cats, and simply being there for the animals who needed comfort. The shelter became his second home—the rows of cages, the smell of newspaper and disinfectant, and the sounds of anxious animals yearning for attention were all familiar to him.

As an only child, Timmy sometimes felt lonely, but he never felt alone when he was with the animals. He understood their pain and longing for love, and he made it his mission to give them as much affection as he could. His favorite book was *The Giving Tree*, and he saw the dogs and cats in the shelter as the tree in the story—giving all they had, asking for nothing in return.

Timmy was especially attentive on the days when the shelter had to make room for new arrivals. These were the hardest days, the days when some of the animals who hadn't found a home were put down to make space for others. Timmy knew what those days meant, and it broke his heart. He couldn't bear the thought of his friends being taken away forever, so he made sure to be there, spending every possible moment with them.

On those somber mornings, Timmy would wake up early, his small hands trembling as he packed his favorite book into his backpack. He would arrive at the shelter before the sun fully rose, the air still crisp and cool. The staff knew him well by then and gave him space to do what he needed to do. He would walk quietly to the cages, one by one, and sit down outside them. With a gentle voice, he would begin to read *The Giving Tree*, his soft words filling the room with warmth and love.

The dogs would sit, their eyes fixed on Timmy, as if they understood every word he was saying. In those moments, there was no fear, no pain—just the connection between a boy and his beloved friends. Timmy would end each reading with a big hug, pressing his cheek against the soft fur of each dog, whispering, "It's going to be alright." He would call them by their names, assuring them that they were about to embark on a journey to their forever home, a place where they would be loved and cared for, where they could run free, healthy, and happy.

What Timmy didn't know was that he was never truly alone in those moments. The Grim Reaper, a dark, ominous figure in a flowing black robe, always sat beside him. The Reaper was there to collect the souls of the dogs, to guide them to the other side. Though Timmy couldn't see him, the Reaper's presence brought a sense of calm and peace to the room. He made sure that the dogs understood Timmy's words, that they knew they were loved and that they were not alone.

As Timmy read, the Reaper would sit quietly next to him, listening to the familiar story. The Reaper had guided many souls from one world to the next, but something about Timmy's pure heart and genuine love for these animals moved him deeply. The Reaper did not agree with the ways of humans—their need to take lives to make space for others—but he was not there to judge. He was there to perform his duty, to collect the souls and ensure they crossed over without pain or fear.

As the shelter staff carried out the sad task, the Reaper would gently take the souls of the animals, sparing them from pain in their final moments. He made sure that their last memories were of Timmy's voice, his warmth, and his love. To the Reaper, these animals were innocent, their only desire was to love and be loved in return.

Timmy kept a journal, meticulously documenting each animal he met, their stories, and the experiences they shared. He took pictures of them, capturing their spirits in a way that made them unforgettable. Over the years, this journal became his most treasured possession—a testament to the love and care he had given to those who needed it most.

As Timmy grew older, his love for animals never wavered. He continued to volunteer at the shelter, doing everything he could to make a difference. Eventually, when he was old enough and his life had settled into a steady rhythm, he adopted a dog of his own—a loyal companion who loved him unconditionally. But even then, he never stopped visiting the shelter, never stopped reading to the animals who waited for a home that might never come.

Years passed, and Timmy's life was filled with love, family, and the companionship of the many animals who had crossed his path. He married, had children, and shared his passion for helping animals with them. His dog, who had been by his side for so many years, grew old and frail. The day came when Timmy knew he had to say goodbye to his beloved friend.

On that final day, as Timmy sat with his dog, he gently stroked its soft fur, whispering, "It's going to be alright, boy," while pressing his cheek against the warm fur, holding his beloved pet close. In that moment, he felt something he hadn't experienced since his days at the shelter—a strong, calming presence filled the room. Though he couldn't see anything, Timmy felt the same peace, the same sense of calm that had always enveloped him on the darkest days at the shelter, return to him once more.

The Reaper took the soul of Timmy's dog, as he had done with so many others before, and Timmy knew his friend was going to a place where there was no pain, only love.

As time passed and Timmy himself grew old, the memories of the animals he had loved and cared for remained with him. His journal, now filled with decades of stories and pictures, was a testament to a life lived with compassion and empathy. Timmy's children and grandchildren would read the stories, understanding the deep love their father and grandfather had for the creatures who had crossed his path.

When Timmy's own time came, he felt no fear. As he drifted into the final sleep, he once again felt the familiar presence. This time, however, he saw him. The Grim Reaper stood at the foot of his bed, tall and imposing, his hooded robe flowing like shadows in the dim light. His face was obscured in darkness, but his presence was not one of menace. The scythe he carried was not raised in threat but held with a sense of solemn duty. Beside him, Timmy saw the shimmering forms of all the animals he had ever loved. Their eyes, filled with the same love and trust he had always known, were there to greet him, to welcome him into the place he had always told them about.

The Reaper spoke, his voice gentle and full of respect. "Timmy," he said, "I have been with you throughout your journey, from the days you spent at the shelter to this very moment. Every soul you touched remembers you. They carry you with them on their journey, just as you carried them in your heart."

With a solemn grace, the Reaper handed Timmy a book. Timmy reached out, his hands trembling slightly as he took it, and instantly recognized the familiar green cover. It was *The Giving Tree*, the book he had read so many times to comfort the animals. A wave of emotion washed over him, knowing that the Reaper had kept it for this moment, so he could read it once more to the souls he had cherished. The animals had loved hearing the story just as much as he had loved reading it to them.

Tears filled Timmy's eyes as he looked at the countless animals gathered around him, their love and gratitude shining brightly. "Thank you," he whispered, his voice filled with emotion.

The Reaper nodded, a suggestion of a smile on his skeletal visage. "It's time to go home, Timmy," he said softly. "You've done well. You've given so much love, and now, it's your turn to receive it."

As Timmy stepped forward, he was enveloped in warmth and light. The souls of the animals surrounded him, their love lifting him, guiding him to the place he had always known was waiting for them all.

In that place beyond the veil, where there was no pain, no suffering, only endless fields and a sky full of light, Timmy found his forever home.

Into the Abyss

DEREK HAD SPENT HIS life chasing the unknown. As a marine biologist and a deep sea explorer, his career was built around the mysteries of the ocean's depths. Each expedition felt like peeling back the layers of an uncharted world. His team, seasoned researchers, ventured into territories few had dared approach, using advanced submersibles to reach the ocean floor and uncover what lay beyond the abyssal plains.

Every mission required weeks of meticulous preparation. The equipment had to withstand the crushing pressures of the deep ocean, and the human body—despite all training—remained fragile in these environments. They had explored past the 200-meter mark regularly, pushing deeper into the seabed where the ocean turned into an alien landscape of towering ridges, craters, and unseen life.

On this particular mission, Derek's team was attempting to descend further than ever before. The pressure gauges creaked as the submersible descended into the darkness, beyond 6,000 meters—toward the edge of the Mariana Trench. The surface was long gone, only blackness encased the vessel as they slipped further into the ocean's depths.

Derek's role was critical: his dive was part of an ongoing project to study life at these unimaginable depths. Yet, no matter how many missions they undertook, time always betrayed them. Their bodies couldn't withstand the pressure for long enough to explore as much as they wanted. Despite discovering bioluminescent creatures and fields of geothermal vents erupting from the seabed, they always had to return too soon. There was so much more to see.

This time was different. As Derek dove beyond the seabed, past 8,000 meters, something went wrong. Alarms blared, his oxygen levels dropped, and the readings on his equipment showed catastrophic failure. The cold crept into his bones, and panic seized his body.

Suddenly, he could feel his pulse slowing. The weight of the water pressed down on him, and though Derek tried to fight, his body was shutting down. And then, as his consciousness began to fade, he saw the figure—a shadow cutting through the ocean's blackness: the Grim Reaper, cloaked and silent, drifting effortlessly in the dark water.

His skeletal face was calm, yet commanding. Derek felt a sudden surge of anger and desperation.

"No," Derek gasped, his voice barely audible. "I'm not done! There's still so much left to explore. I haven't even seen half of what's down here!"

The Reaper didn't speak, but Derek felt the answer in his mind, like a ripple through the water: *It is not your choice.*

The pressure on his body faded, and as Derek's soul began to separate from his physical form, the Reaper gently extended his hand. There was no malice in the gesture, only inevitability. Derek's protests were swallowed by the stillness of the deep, and soon, his soul passed from the world of the living.

But death was not what Derek had expected.

In the ethereal realm, he found himself submerged in darkness, as deep and endless as the ocean itself. Yet, through this abyss, a light began to break through. Shapes and shadows emerged from the black void—lifeforms unlike any Derek had seen during his dives. There were colossal creatures and vibrant, luminous beings, weaving through forests of underwater plants. The very seafloor teemed with vibrant life, pulsing with colors that human eyes could never perceive.

He felt no pressure, no need for air. There were no limits anymore. He swam freely through the oceanic landscape, exploring the depths of the world he could never fully reach in life. Every moment was filled with discovery, and with each new revelation, Derek felt a deep sense of peace.

The Grim Reaper stayed by his side, watching silently. Derek understood now. This—this wondrous, flourishing world—was always beyond his reach in life, and no amount of diving deeper or preparing more could have changed that. He wasn't meant to experience it while alive. This was the place where he belonged.

Eternal Waters

It was a perfect day in the ocean. The water was crystal clear, shimmering under the sun's rays, and Joey swam alongside his mother, weaving through the gentle waves. They moved with grace, their sleek black-and-white bodies cutting effortlessly through the cool, blue depths. The distinctive white patches above Joey's eyes stood out as he darted through beams of sunlight, small fish scattering in his wake. Joey was still young, his body small but strong, and every movement was filled with energy and joy. His mother swam close, her presence comforting and protective. They were happy, and the ocean was their playground.

As Joey and his mother surfaced for air, they noticed something unfamiliar. A distant rumble grew louder, and the peaceful rhythm of the ocean was interrupted. A ship was approaching. At first, neither of them paid much attention, but as the vessel drew closer, panic set in. Without warning, nets were cast into the water, and Joey found himself ensnared.

He thrashed and fought, but the more he struggled, the tighter the net became. His mother swam frantically beside him, calling out, but she too was helpless. Joey could hear her cries—filled with fear and sadness—but the ship was already pulling him out of the water. The last thing he saw was his mother's eyes, full of sorrow, as the ship carried him away.

The men on the ship loaded Joey into a small tank, separating him from the only world he had ever known. He didn't understand that this would be the last time he would see his mother. The ship's rumbling drowned out everything, leaving Joey in cold, silent isolation.

Years passed, and Joey's life was no longer the vast, open ocean. Instead, he was confined to a small enclosure, performing tricks for cheering crowds. At first, he did what was expected of him, hoping it would bring some sense of purpose, but every day he thought about the ocean—about the freedom he once had, and the mother he had lost.

Decades went by. Joey grew older, his spirit quieter. The enclosure became smaller, the crowds seemed distant, and he could hear another orca performing the same tricks he used to. But Joey was no longer part of that world. He was placed in an even smaller tank, left to swim in solitude. His body was tired, and so was his heart.

As Joey floated still in the water one day, his thoughts drifted to the life he had before. He wondered if he would ever be free again, if he would ever see his mother. He missed her, and he missed the ocean. Closing his eyes, Joey felt something change. The water around him grew calm, and then he heard a voice.

"Joey, it's time."

The Grim Reaper appeared beside him, his presence gentle yet commanding. He didn't frighten Joey. Instead, he brought with him a sense of peace.

"The question you've asked for so many years—you'll finally have your answer. You'll know what it's like to be free again. To swim with your mother. Open your eyes, Joey. Swim with me—I have something to show you."

Joey opened his eyes, and to his amazement, he was no longer in the small tank. He was in the ocean, surrounded by open water. It was vast, boundless, and for a moment, Joey didn't understand how he had gotten there. All he remembered was the small enclosure, the loneliness, the years of captivity. But now, here he was—free.

With a burst of joy, Joey began to swim like he had never swum before. He flipped, dove, and raced through the water, feeling alive for the first time in decades. He felt like his old self again, his body strong and full of energy. As he swam, he noticed a figure in the distance. It was familiar.

His mother.

She was swimming toward him, her movements graceful and filled with the same joy he felt. They met in the water, swimming around each other, reunited after so many years apart. Joey and his mother played joyfully, just as they had when he was a young calf, free in the open ocean.

The Grim Reaper watched them from afar, content in their happiness. Joey and his mother swam away together, never to be separated again. They didn't know that they had passed from one life to the next. In this new existence, they would always be together, free to swim in an endless ocean, where no one would ever hurt them again.

Paths Unwritten

Every choice we make has the power to shape our journey and the journeys of those around us.

The Bridge

THE RAIN FELL IN steady sheets, drumming against the wooden planks of the old bridge as Hazel stood there, staring into the river below. Her hands trembled, though whether from the cold or from the weight of her decision, she wasn't sure. The water beneath churned with a wild intensity, its depths unknown and beckoning.

She had walked out here in the dead of night, her footsteps echoing against the hollow bridge, unnoticed by the world around her. The stormy sky was a reflection of her own turmoil, dark and restless. She gripped the railing tightly, her knuckles white, her breath coming in shallow bursts.

Headlights pierced the darkness in the distance, cutting through the rain. A car. It was getting closer. Panic surged through her chest—if she didn't act now, whoever was driving would stop her. Her resolve, firm but fragile, couldn't face an interruption.

Before she could think twice, her feet left the wooden planks. The wind tore at her dress as she fell, the sound of her heartbeat roaring in her ears.

Time stilled.

She wasn't in the water. She wasn't falling. She was suspended in the space between—neither here nor there. Hazel opened her eyes, and instead of the river's cold embrace, she found herself on another bridge. This one stretched across an unending horizon. On one side was peace so profound it made her heart ache; on the other, a gray void of aimless wandering.

And there he was, standing on the bridge, his form indistinct yet palpable. He radiated not warmth but something akin to understanding.

"Why?" Hazel's voice cracked, her words trembling in the air like fragile glass.

He did not answer with words. The Reaper's presence pressed against her like a wave of feeling—empathy, patience, and something she hadn't expected: hope.

"I thought I was ready," she confessed, sinking to her knees on the wooden planks. "I thought this was my choice to make. But I'm not ready. I ... I understand now." Her voice faltered as regret poured from her in ragged sobs.

The Reaper tilted his head, as though studying her. He listened, offering neither judgment nor pity. For the first time, Hazel didn't feel alone.

From the bridge, she could hear a distant voice, faint and frantic, calling out to her. She recognized it—a tether to the life she thought she had left behind. It called her back, pulling her from the in-between.

As she began to rise through the cold water, the bridge blurred. Her connection to the other side began to dissolve, fading like morning mist.

"I'm not ready," she whispered one last time.

The Reaper nodded, a silent acknowledgment that echoed louder than words. He did not move to stop her. He did not guide her forward.

And as Hazel felt hands pulling her from the icy water of the river below, the Reaper turned, shaking his head softly. He lingered for a moment longer, watching as the life she had nearly surrendered began to return. Then he vanished into the gloom of the storm, leaving her to the fate she had reclaimed.

Fates Passing

THE RAIN CAME DOWN in relentless sheets, blurring the edges of Jackson's headlights as he navigated the narrow road. The windshield wipers struggled to keep up, their rhythmic squeaking barely cutting through the drum of rain on the roof. He tightened his grip on the wheel, muttering under his breath about the storm. It was late, and he'd hoped to be home by now, but a detour had added more time to his drive.

As he approached the old wooden bridge, something caught his eye through the rain-streaked windshield. A figure stood at the center of the bridge, barely illuminated by the faint glow of his headlights. His heart kicked in his chest.

A woman.

Her dress clung to her, soaked and fluttering in the wind. She stood motionless, her hair plastered against her face, her arms wrapped around herself as if shielding against the cold.

"What is she doing out here?" Jackson whispered, easing off the gas.

The car crept closer, his headlights now fully casting their light on her. She turned her head ever so slightly, just enough for him to see her face, pale and rain-soaked. Her eyes met his for the briefest of moments, filled with a mix of fear and resolve.

Before he could even think to react, she stepped forward—and disappeared over the side of the bridge.

"No!" Jackson slammed on the brakes, the tires skidding slightly before the car came to a halt at the far end of the bridge. He fumbled to throw it into park, his hands shaking. His heart pounded as he reached for his phone on the passenger seat and shoved open the door, leaving it ajar as he stumbled out into the rain.

His boots splashed against the wet ground as he ran toward the riverbank, his breath coming in gasps. "Where are you?" he called, his voice nearly lost in the storm.

He reached the edge and looked down. The water churned violently, the current strong and unforgiving. For a moment, he froze, his eyes scanning the darkness, searching for any sign of her. Then he saw it—a faint outline, her body caught in the river's pull.

Without hesitation, Jackson tossed his phone to the ground and dove in.

The cold water hit him like a wall, stealing the breath from his lungs. He kicked against the current, pushing himself toward her. His fingers brushed fabric, and then her arm, limp and cold. Gritting his teeth, he wrapped his arms around her and fought his way back to the shore, his muscles burning with every stroke.

When his feet finally found solid ground, Jackson heaved her onto the muddy bank and collapsed beside her, gasping for air. She wasn't moving.

"No, no, no," he murmured, leaning over her. Her face was pale, her lips blue, and for a terrifying moment, he thought he was too late. But then he felt it—a faint pulse beneath his trembling fingers.

"Come on," he urged, tilting her head back and pressing his ear close to her mouth. A shallow breath ghosted against his skin. Relief surged through him, but it was fleeting. She needed more help than he could give.

Jackson scrambled for his phone, slipping in the mud as he dialed with shaking fingers. "I need help! A woman jumped off the bridge—she's barely breathing!" His voice broke as he gave his location, his eyes never leaving her still form.

The storm raged around them, the world a blur of water and darkness. Jackson could not feel the shadow that lingered just beyond the reach of the headlights.

The Grim Reaper watched in silence, his form indistinct in the foggy night. He hovered at the edge of the scene, unseen and unnoticed. For a moment, he remained still, observing the fragile thread of life hanging in the balance.

The Reaper would wait.

Whisper Between Worlds

In the quiet space between life and death, love reminds us that connection endures beyond boundaries.

The Silent Plea

Grayson's car hung precariously off the edge of the mountain, its front end wrapped tightly around a large tree that had stopped her from plummeting further. The once sleek silver vehicle was now crumpled, the windshield shattered, and the driver-side door bent inward from the force of the crash. The headlights flickered in the early evening light, their dim glow casting long shadows across the ground, while the faint smell of burning rubber filled the air. Beyond the twisted metal, the landscape stretched out in a peaceful display of nature—pine trees swaying gently in the wind, the sound of a distant river flowing through the valley, and a setting sun that would soon take the light of day with it.

Inside the car, Grayson lay unconscious, her dark hair tangled and splayed across the dashboard. Her face, though bruised and marked from the crash, still held a striking beauty—a delicate expression that seemed to belong to someone far too kind and gentle for the world she had been living in. Her chest rose and fell unevenly, her breath shallow as she teetered between life and death.

Beside her, in the passenger seat of the car, sat the Grim Reaper.

The interior of the car was silent, except for the quiet creak of the metal frame. The Grim Reaper's black robe draped across the torn seat, his skeletal hand gripping the scythe that rested against his shoulder. For a moment, he simply watched Grayson, his hooded figure still and foreboding. Yet, as he looked at her, there was no malice in his presence—only a quiet reflection. Grayson's innocence and beauty struck him deeply, something about her different from the countless souls he had guided before. Her long, dark hair framed a face etched with sorrow, and though the physical wounds from the crash were apparent, it was the deeper wounds—the ones that had festered within her for years—that drew his attention.

The Reaper had seen pain in many forms, but Grayson's was different. It wasn't just the physical pain from the crash that stirred something within him—it was the pain that had woven its way through her life, the heartbreak, the loneliness, the unfulfilled yearning for love.

As he gazed at her, he saw everything. He saw her life unfold before him in an instant—her tireless efforts to be the perfect partner, her constant pursuit of love, always giving more of herself than she ever received in return. He saw the way she had danced when she was younger, her joy in singing alone in her room, and how all of that had slowly faded over time as heartbreak after heartbreak dimmed her spirit. Now, she was quiet—too quiet. She no longer sang, no longer danced, no longer believed that she was enough. The Reaper felt the weight of her despair, and he knew that if he left her to survive, she would return to the same cycle of pain.

He wished he could make things different for her, make it so that she wouldn't have to suffer anymore. He had never wanted anything like this before. As he watched her, he could hear her thoughts, her soul crying out to him in its pain, begging for release.

Grayson, he spoke to her mind, his voice not carried on sound but in a feeling—a presence. *You are in between, hovering between life and death. I feel the heaviness of your soul. I know the hurt you've carried for so long.*

Without any movement, they were no longer in the crumpled car. They were sitting at the top of the mountain, high above the valley where the river snaked through the trees. The sky was darkening, the air cool and serene. Grayson was there beside him, silent, but he felt her thoughts as clearly as if they were his own. She didn't want to return to her life. She was tired—tired of the fight, tired of never being enough, tired of the endless heartache. She wanted to stay with the Reaper. She wanted the Reaper to take her soul and let her be free from the weight of living.

But the Reaper, though moved by her plea, could not grant her wish.

Grayson, he whispered in her mind again, *I have to send you back. It is not your time. There is still love waiting for you, still a life you need to live. You are tired, I know. But this is not the end for you. Go fall in love. Feel the things you've denied yourself because of the pain. I will be with you, but I cannot take you now.*

Her soul wept, pleading to stay, to let her remain in this peaceful place where nothing hurt, where she didn't have to face the world again. She leaned against him, resting her head on his shoulder as they sat together in the fading light. It was quiet, peaceful, and for the first time in a long while, she felt a sense of comfort and love—love that didn't demand anything from her.

Just a little longer, she thought, and the Reaper allowed it. He let her stay in this in-between space, hovering between life and death. Down below, rescue workers were frantically trying to extract her from the wreckage, unaware that Grayson's soul was sitting on the mountain, resisting the pull of life.

They sat together, watching the world below, the sun casting a soft glow on the horizon. Grayson closed her eyes, savoring the calm, the sense of belonging she felt in that moment. But when she opened them again, she was no longer on the mountain. She was in a hospital bed, the room dim and quiet, the beeping of machines softly echoing in the background. He had sent her back. She was alive and awake, her body fragile but healing. She didn't speak, but she understood. She kept her eyes on him, knowing he would soon be gone.

The Reaper was there, standing in the corner, watching over her silently. He had given her the chance to love again, to find the happiness that had always eluded her, even though it wasn't what she wanted. And though her heart ached for the peace of the in-between, she knew he was right.

You have returned, he told her silently. *I will always be by your side when you feel lost, there to catch you when you fall. But your journey is far from over. Love will find you.*

And with that, the Reaper faded from her view, leaving Grayson in the quiet hospital room with something different stirring in her heart. He would return when the time was right, but until then, she had a life to live—and love to find—before their paths crossed again.

The Silent Embrace

GRAYSON SAT QUIETLY ON a park bench one evening, the chill in the air matching the sadness she felt deep inside. The sun was sinking below the horizon, casting a soft glow on the world around her. She wasn't sure why, but she always felt as though someone was watching over her. Not in the way that made her feel unsafe, but in a way that comforted her, almost like a presence that had been with her during her hardest times. And tonight, she could feel it more than ever.

Unbeknownst to her, the Grim Reaper was near, watching her from a distance. He had been visiting her often since the accident, drawn to her in a way that left him perplexed. It wasn't just her beauty—though her long dark hair framed her face like shadows embracing the moon, and the elegant structure of her cheeks hinted at the artistry of the bones beneath. No, it was something deeper. He had never felt this before, this pull toward a human soul, this desire to protect her. He wanted to be near her, to feel what it might be like to love. But he knew, no matter how much he wanted it, it was impossible. He was the Reaper, bound by duties that could never be broken.

Grayson glanced around, her heart heavy. She didn't understand why, but she sensed something. It wasn't a sound or a sight, but a feeling, a presence she couldn't explain. She closed her eyes, her thoughts drifting, and as she did, she felt him—there but untouchable. He spoke to her without words, his presence comforting her sadness.

I'm here, he told her silently.

She didn't reply with words, but she felt him too, and somehow, she knew he was there for her. Their connection, though unspoken, was undeniable. They were worlds apart, yet in these brief moments, they were closer than ever.

The Reaper longed to reach out and touch her, to feel what humans felt, to comfort her in a way that was beyond his reach. He admired the way her dark hair fell over her shoulders, the way her eyes held a quiet sadness, and how, even in her sorrow, she radiated a gentle strength. He wished he could take her away from all of it, to give her peace. But he knew he couldn't. He was not meant for that kind of life.

As they sat together in silence, the evening slowly fading into night, Grayson felt a strange comfort in his presence. She didn't know why or how, but she didn't feel alone. She felt cared for, watched over, and in some small way, loved.

I wish I could stay with you forever, the Reaper thought, but he knew it was not possible.

Grayson's heart ached, and she leaned her head back against the bench, closing her eyes again. She didn't know what she was feeling, only that it gave her a strange sense of peace. She spoke to him without words, and he responded in kind, their bond growing in the silence between them.

I will always be with you, he communicated softly, though he knew they could never truly be together.

In that moment, as they shared the quiet peace of the evening, the Reaper understood his longing. He wanted what humans had—the ability to touch, to love, to be close to someone in a way that went beyond the ethereal.

Grayson felt the sadness in him, the distance that could never be bridged. She too longed for more, but deep down, she knew the truth.

Before he left her, he did something he had never done before—he wrapped his arms around her, pulling her into a silent embrace. Grayson felt it, the warmth of his presence enveloping her, a comfort she had longed for but had never found. In that hug, there was no pain, no sadness, only a deep sense of peace.

Until we meet again, the Reaper thought, his arms slowly releasing her as the night grew darker. Grayson, still unaware of how many times he had visited her or how often he stood by her side, simply felt the comfort of his presence fading. She would never know how often he watched over her, but he would always carry that knowledge, visiting her in the silence, watching, protecting, longing for what could never be.

The Dance

THE MOON HUNG HIGH above the city, its pale light spilling over the balcony where Grayson stood. The gentle breath of the evening breeze carried the muted sounds of distant conversations, mingling with the hum of the city below. Tonight, she wore a simple dress that flowed like water around her as she swayed to the music playing softly in her apartment. The melody wasn't from a radio or speaker—it was a song she hummed quietly to herself, one that brought her peace and made her feel close to him.

Grayson moved gracefully, her body flowing with an unspoken rhythm. Her movements were fluid, as if she were dancing with an unseen partner. She imagined strong arms guiding her, twirling her, holding her close. Her heart ached, not with longing, but with a quiet joy that came from the depth of her love.

Suddenly, a familiar warmth enveloped her. It was subtle at first—a sensation she had felt before, a presence that had become both a comfort and a mystery. She opened her eyes, but the balcony was empty. Still, she knew he was there.

"I feel you," she whispered into the night.

In response, the breeze shifted, swirling around her, and she felt it—his touch. The Reaper's presence was no longer distant. She turned, and for the first time, she felt him fully, as though he had stepped from the shadows into her world. He was not visible in the way a man might be, but she could feel the solidity of him, the warmth of his hand as he took hers and spun her gently.

As they danced under the stars, the city lights below twinkling like tiny lanterns, he took her back—not in memory, but in sensation. She was there again, atop the mountain where they had first met. The air was cool and crisp, the sun setting in hues of gold and crimson over the valley. She could feel the peace of that moment, the quiet understanding they had shared.

"I sat with you there," the Reaper said, his voice heavy with emotion. "I felt your pain, your sorrow. I wanted to take it all away, to bring you peace. But more than that, I wanted to give you the chance to find love. I told you that love was waiting for you, not knowing then that it would be ... me."

Grayson's breath caught in her throat. "You?" she whispered. "You are the love you spoke of?"

"Yes," he confessed, his presence trembling with vulnerability. "You have shown me what it is to love, to care for another in a way I never thought possible. And though I cannot be with you in the way I wish, know that my very being is yours."

Tears glistened in her eyes as she rested her head against his chest. The stars above seemed to shimmer brighter, their glow illuminating the moment with a quiet radiance. "I never thought I could feel this," she said softly. "To be loved so completely, so selflessly. You've shown me that love can heal even the deepest wounds."

There was no music to guide their steps, only the gentle hum of her melody carried on the breeze, binding them in a harmony no song could replicate. For what felt like hours, they danced, their movements slow and deliberate, their connection transcending the boundaries of life and death.

In his arms, she felt safe, cherished, and whole. And for the Reaper, holding her was a gift he had never known he could desire.

When the night began to fade into the pale blush of dawn, he knew he had to leave. But this time, he lingered, his form reluctant to fade. "I don't want to go," he admitted, his voice heavy with sorrow.

Grayson placed a gentle hand on where his cheek might have been, her touch filled with understanding. "I know," she said softly. "But I will be here, always. And I will always love you."

With one final twirl, he released her, his presence fading into the night. But the warmth of his touch, the memory of their dance, stayed with her, a promise that their connection would never truly end.

The Final Farewell

THE EVENING WAS WARM, with a gentle breeze carrying the soft scent of blooming jasmine into Grayson's cozy home. The air was filled with the sound of laughter and soft music, mingling with the clinking of glasses as Grayson sat on her porch, her head tilted back in a carefree laugh that lit up her entire face. Across from her, a man leaned in, his smile wide and filled with affection. His hand brushed hers gently, their fingers meeting with an ease that spoke of a tender connection.

Unseen by either of them, the Grim Reaper stood just beyond the porch, his form blending into the stillness of the evening. But tonight, he felt no sense of duty pulling him toward her. Instead, he felt something unfamiliar—an ache that spread through him as he watched Grayson with the man who now brought her the joy he had wished for her since he met her.

She's happy. That was all that mattered. As much as it pained him, the Reaper knew that this was how it was meant to be. Grayson deserved this—a life filled with love, laughter, and companionship. He had given her the chance to find it, and she had taken it, as he had hoped she would.

But the ache did not subside. He lingered, watching as she leaned closer to the man, her eyes sparkling with a light he had never seen before. Her laughter was like music, and though it warmed him to know she had found this happiness, it also broke something deep within him.

He knew he could not stay. His presence would only disrupt the life she was building, the love she was learning to embrace. Grayson had to live her life fully, without the shadow of his visits holding her back. With one last look, the Reaper turned away, fading into the night.

Years passed. The Reaper never visited her again. He stayed away, though she was never far from his thoughts. He imagined her laughing, dancing, and growing older with a family of her own. He found solace in the idea that she was living the life she deserved. Yet, on nights when the world felt particularly heavy, he thought of her. Her smile, her warmth, the way she had once looked at him as if she could truly see him.

And then, one day, he felt the pull. It was her time.

The hospital room was quiet, save for the soft hum of machines and the muted whispers of her family. Grayson lay in the center of it all, her hair now silver and soft, draped delicately across the pillow. Her face, once framed by the dark curls he had admired, was now lined with the years she had lived. Yet, to him, she was more beautiful than ever. Her bone structure remained regal, her eyes no longer full of longing but of peace and fulfillment. She looked different, but she was still Grayson—the woman who had changed him.

Around her stood her husband, her children, and her grandchildren, their love filling the room as they held her hands, whispered words of comfort, and wiped away their tears. Grayson's heart was content and ready. Though she wanted to stay for them, she knew she could not. She felt hopeful that she would see the Reaper again, but this time, she did not long to leave the world. She had lived a full life, and though it was difficult to let go, she knew it was her time.

The Reaper appeared, stepping silently into the room. He felt the weight of his duty as he looked at her, frail but still so beautiful, her spirit glowing brightly even as her body faded. The warmth of her presence hit him like a wave, the same warmth he had felt all those years ago. But this time, it was different. It was the warmth of a life well lived, a heart that had loved deeply and been loved in return.

This was not how he had imagined this moment. Life—her life—had changed that. He had always known they could never truly be together, but a small part of him had hoped. He had wished for something impossible. Yet, he knew better. He always had.

Grayson stirred, her eyes fluttering open. Though she couldn't see him, she felt him—just as she always had. A soft smile graced her lips as she looked beyond her family, her gaze settling where he stood.

"You're here," she whispered, her voice weak but filled with a quiet joy.

"I am," he replied, his voice a gentle caress in her mind. "It's time, Grayson."

She nodded, her eyes glistening with tears, though not from fear or sadness. "I've missed you," she said softly.

The Reaper knelt beside her, his presence wrapping around her like a warm embrace. "I never forgot you," he admitted. "There were times I wanted to see you, to feel your presence again, but I knew it would only hurt us both. Watching you laugh and love from afar was enough for me, knowing you were happy."

The Reaper placed a hand over her heart, feeling the steady slowing of its beat. "And I never forgot you," he said. "All of our memories will always be with me, and you will carry them with you. My heart is breaking again, but it has been an honor to know you, Grayson. You've changed me in ways I cannot explain."

Grayson's gaze shifted to her husband and their children, her heart swelling with gratitude and pride. "They're my everything," she said, her voice trembling with emotion. "But I never forgot you. Not once."

As her final breath escaped her lips, the Reaper gently gathered her soul, a radiant light that shimmered with all the love and memories of her life. He watched as she turned to him one last time, her essence glowing with gratitude and peace.

"Goodbye," she said, her voice like a melody carried on the wind.

"Goodbye, Grayson," he replied, his heart breaking again even as he smiled. "You were my light in the shadows."

And with that, he released her, watching as her soul ascended to join the eternal, where love and peace awaited her. The room grew quiet, and the Reaper stood alone once more, the weight of his duty settling over him.

But as he faded into the shadows, he carried her memory with him, a piece of her light that would guide him through the darkness. For though their paths had finally parted, she would remain with him forever, a love that transcended time and space.

The Fragile Horizon

To face mortality is to see the beauty and fragility of life with greater clarity.

Light in the Darkness

FRANCINE LAY IN HER bed, her gaze fixed on the night sky outside her window. The room was silent, with only the faint ticking of the clock on the wall breaking the stillness. The darkness outside seemed so inviting, yet within it, she saw more than just the absence of light. She saw every detail illuminated, as if the silhouettes of the night shone with a radiant light of their own. It was a contradiction she had come to know well—the darkness that seemed to offer solace, but in reality, was filled with an eerie glow, pulling her toward despair.

For years, Francine had battled the darkness within herself. The whispers that crept into her mind told her that life was too hard, that she wasn't worth the love she craved. Those voices, always so persuasive, had led her down paths she wished she'd never taken. They told her she was brave, that she could end her pain if she just took that final step. And each time, she did.

She remembered the first time she tried to end her life. The voices had been particularly convincing that day, whispering that death was a release, a way to escape the endless cycle of pain and disappointment. She had felt an unbearable, sharp pain in her chest, and then the world around her had blurred as she crumpled to the floor, blood pooling beneath her. But as the darkness closed in, the relief she had hoped for never came. Instead, she found herself face to face with a figure cloaked in black, his skeletal hand gripping a scythe that glimmered faintly in the dim light.

The Grim Reaper stood before her, his presence imposing but not malevolent. His face was hidden beneath the hood of his robe, but his voice was clear, resonating in her mind.

"Francine," he said softly, his voice a mix of sadness and understanding, "this is not your time. You are not meant to die today."

Francine had felt a deep sense of remorse as she lay there, her body broken, but her spirit still tethered to life. She tried to speak, but the words wouldn't come. The Reaper didn't need her to speak; he could sense her regret, her fear.

"You are needed in this world," he continued, his voice filled with a quiet authority. "There are people who love you, who need you. Your purpose is not yet fulfilled. I will see you again one day. It's time for you to go back."

With that, the Reaper touched her lightly on the forehead, and Francine felt herself being pulled back into the world of the living. When she awoke, she was in a hospital bed, her heart beating weakly but steadily. The voices were gone for a time, but the darkness still lingered at the edges of her consciousness, waiting for another moment of weakness.

This pattern repeated itself over the years. Each time Francine attempted to end her life, the voices urged her on, telling her it was the only way to find peace. And each time, the Reaper would appear. He reminded her of her worth, of the love that still existed in the world, even if she couldn't see it. And each time, he sent her back with a message of hope and a reminder that her time had not yet come.

But the voices were relentless. They told her she was alone, that no one cared, that the pain would never end. They whispered lies that felt like truths, twisting her thoughts, convincing her that the only escape was to surrender to the darkness. And so, she attempted to silence the torment in various ways, each more desperate than the last, hoping to find peace in the void.

The Reaper's visits became more frequent, each one more intense than the last. He would stand before her, his dark robes flowing around him like shadows come to life, his scythe a constant reminder of the finality she sought. Yet, despite his grim appearance, there was a warmth in his presence, a kindness she didn't expect.

"Francine," he would say, his tone firmer, "you are stronger than you know. The world is a better place with you in it. You have a purpose, a reason to be here. Don't let these lost souls deceive you. They are trapped in their own darkness and want to pull you into it with them. But you must resist. Your life is precious, and there is still so much for you to do."

Francine would cry each time, apologizing for her weakness, for giving in to the voices. The Reaper would place a comforting hand on her shoulder, his touch gentle despite the coldness of his skeletal fingers.

"It's not your time," he would repeat, sending her back once more.

The final attempt came on a night much like any other. The voices were louder than ever, insistent, pushing her to the brink. Desperation consumed her, and she made yet another attempt to end the pain, hoping that this time, she would finally find peace. As her consciousness began to fade, she glimpsed the familiar figure of the Reaper standing over her.

But this time, there was something different. The Reaper's demeanor had changed. He seemed almost ... relieved.

"This is the last time I will come to you like this," he said softly. "You have faced the darkness so many times, but it is still not your time to leave this world. You have learned, finally, that you are stronger than the voices that haunt you. They no longer have power over you."

Francine felt a shift within herself, a realization that had been building slowly over time. She had begun to see the voices for what they were—manipulations, lies, and shadows that fed on her pain. With this newfound clarity, she summoned the courage to reject them, to recognize that her thoughts were her own and that her life had value.

Sensing her strength, the Reaper nodded, his hand sweeping through the air in a gentle, yet decisive motion. The spirits that had tormented her for so long began to fade, their grip on her loosening as they were banished from her life. But it was Francine's own resolve that truly severed their hold.

"They are gone now," he told her. "You are free from their influence. It's time for you to live your life—to find the joy and the love that you deserve. One day, we will meet again, but that day is far from now. Until then, live, Francine. Live and find your light in the darkness."

As the Reaper's words resonated in her mind, Francine felt a sense of peace wash over her. For the first time in years, the darkness no longer felt suffocating. It was just the night—calm, still, and filled with the promise of a new day.

From that day forward, Francine embraced life with a renewed sense of purpose. The voices never returned, and she knew that the Reaper had given her a gift—a second chance to live fully and without fear. She knew that he was out there, watching over her, ensuring that she would live to see the light of many more days. Often, she found herself gazing out into the night sky, once a source of dread, now one of calm and beauty. Where others might see only darkness, Francine saw light—a reflection of the peace she had found within herself, and a reminder that even in the darkest times, there is always light to guide the way.

The Light of Day

Andrew stood at the side of the stage, guitar in hand, waiting for his cue. The crowd began to cheer, clapping and calling out the name everyone knew him by, "Droo." He stepped onto the stage in his sneakers, wearing his signature plain T-shirt, jean shorts and a flowery guitar strap that had become a part of his persona. His long hair was tied back, and his presence exuded a laid-back, '60s vibe that everyone adored.

Though he played many instruments, the guitar was his favorite. His music had a way of reaching people, connecting with their emotions, and he was known not just for his songs but for the kindness he showed to those around him. He mentored young musicians, wrote songs that spoke of life, love, and the mysteries of existence, and always made time for his fans.

That night's performance was something special, though Droo had no way of knowing just how much it would come to mean. His friends and fans filled the audience, and at the side of the stage, his dog, L'il Stoney, sat faithfully, never missing a show. The routine at the end was always the same—he would grab L'il Stoney, sit on the edge of the stage as the crowd began to disperse, and then spend time with those who had come to see him, taking pictures, sharing stories, and building connections that would last a lifetime.

After the show, Droo packed up his equipment, and with L'il Stoney by his side, they hit the road. As usual, he called his mom on the drive home, recounting the night's events, sharing stories, and enjoying the comfort of her voice. He was always careful as he drove home; he had an important passenger to keep safe.

In the days that followed, Droo began to feel unwell. What started as fatigue and an unshakable fever soon spiraled into sharp pains in his chest and difficulty breathing. A visit to the hospital quickly escalated into a situation far more serious than he could have imagined. He found himself lying in a hospital bed, surrounded by doctors and nurses, in the sterile environment of a place he had never expected to be. The days dragged on, each one a battle, and Droo, ill and on a lot of medication, drifted between dreams and memories—his shows, his family, his loyal dog, his friends, and his fans. He couldn't tell if he was dreaming or remembering, but he clung to those moments as if they were all he had left.

One evening, as the quiet hum of the hospital surrounded him, a voice called his name. It was unfamiliar, soft, almost … a whisper. "Andrew, it's showtime. There are people waiting for you. They have things to say, things you need to hear." He opened his eyes and found himself no longer in the hospital bed but standing, fully dressed in a suit—a rare occurrence, reserved only for special occasions. The Grim Reaper stood before him, a calm presence.

"Are you ready?" the Reaper asked, turning away as Droo nodded, a quiet *"Yes"* escaping his lips. They passed through the hospital room door as if it wasn't there, and suddenly, Droo was surrounded by his friends, his family, and his beloved L'il Stoney, sitting on his mom's lap. There were pictures of him, music playing, and people sharing memories. He listened as they spoke about him, celebrating his life, his music, and the impact he had on them. It was a tribute to all he had been, and as he stood there, watching, it filled him with a deep sadness.

The Reaper, sensing Droo's pain, spoke softly. "You were taken too soon, Andrew. You weren't ready, and neither were they. But I want you to see that even though you've left this world, you still remain. Your music, your kindness—they've left a mark that time cannot erase. I want you to witness it, to experience the light of day through their lives."

With that, the Reaper disappeared, leaving Droo in a place where time seemed to stretch and bend. He watched over his loved ones as they remembered him, honored him, dreamt of him, and spoke to him in moments of quiet reflection. He was there with them, letting them know in subtle ways that he was still listening, still there by their side.

Years passed, but for Droo, time was different. Droo watched his friends and family grow old, but they never forgot him. He knew that when the time came, the Reaper would visit each one. He worried about what would happen, and braced himself, for he had grown accustomed to watching over them, to being a part of their lives from this place between worlds.

One day, as Droo watched L'il Stoney climb into his bed for what would be the last time, the Reaper appeared again. Droo saw the tiny soul leave his dog's body, and in an instant, the bright light of the afterlife began to shine. A small furry figure came running toward him, and Droo crouched down, opening his arms wide. With one joyful leap, L'il Stoney was in his arms, licking his face with pure happiness.

"Welcome home, boy!" Droo shouted with excitement, holding his little friend close.

From that moment, Droo and L'il Stoney continued to watch over their loved ones. As each one was visited by the Reaper, Droo knew that they would soon be reunited. And one by one, they were. The Reaper brought each soul to Droo, until the very last one had crossed over from the world Droo had left behind so many years ago.

When the time came, the Reaper guided them all together into a beautiful ray of light. Droo, with his mother by his side and L'il Stoney in her arms, his family, and friends, walked into the light, feeling a sense of peace and completeness he had never known before.

Droo's music continued to play on, echoing through the years, a lasting reminder of the love and joy he left in the world. Though he was gone, he was never forgotten.

An Inexplicable Calm

THE GRIM REAPER'S PRESENCE was not unfamiliar to Giselle. Their paths had first crossed when she was a mere eight years old. During a summer camp outing, Giselle's lifeless body sank deeper into the murky depths of the lake. As her soul left her body, the Reaper appeared beside her in the water. His voice, though silent, resonated in her mind: *Giselle, open your eyes. I should not be here with you. It is not your time. Your life has just begun; there is much more for you to do and experience in this world. You are meant to do good and make a difference in many lives. You have a greater purpose to fulfill.* With this message delivered, the Reaper vanished, leaving Giselle to soon awaken and return to the life she was destined to live.

Although confused, Giselle felt an inexplicable calm. Time around her seemed to stretch and bend, the moments underwater feeling much longer than they truly were. Meanwhile, on the lake's shore, a frantic rescue effort was underway. Giselle's lifeless body had been retrieved from the water, and a camp counselor was performing CPR, doing her best to try and bring her back to life. After a few minutes, Giselle's heartbeat returned, and she awoke, coughing and gasping for air. Her small body was drenched, but she was alive. The other campers watched in shock, worried at first, then celebrated her miraculous return.

This experience left a lifelong impression on Giselle. She was too young to fully grasp what had happened, but the encounter with the Reaper instilled a lasting sense of peace within her. She knew her time would come, and she would one day see the Reaper again.

Throughout her life, Giselle never forgot the Reaper's words. She understood that she had a greater purpose and was determined to make a positive impact on the world. Her life became a testament to doing good, dedicating herself to helping others and making a difference wherever she could.

Years later, Giselle lay on her kitchen floor, her life slipping away. Memories of her life flooded her mind. A stunning woman with long, dark hair and flawless skin, her beauty remained untouched by time. Her face, even now, reflected a serene acceptance of her fate. She had lived a life rich with experiences, filled with both joy and sorrow, and she had no regrets.

Giselle's life had been filled with valuable lessons. She knew the sting of poverty and the comfort of wealth. Through hard work, she learned to stand on her own, never relying on others. She experienced the thrill of first love, the pain of heartbreak, falling in love all over again, and the bliss of being deeply cherished.

Giselle dedicated her life to helping people and animals, extending kindness to all. Her love surpassed the ordinary, understanding that love is not confined to loving or being loved by one person but is felt through the collective warmth and compassion of everyone around you.

Giselle's childhood experience helped her understand that life was fleeting and death inevitable. Her brief encounter with the Reaper at age eight had taught her not to fear death. This understanding allowed her to embrace life fully, without fear of its end. The peace she felt from that moment never left her, guiding her through life's ups and downs.

Now, as her heart began to fail, the Reaper appeared once more. "Hello, Giselle. It's been a while. Now it's time. I am here to escort you to the afterlife. You have lived a wonderful life, fulfilling your purpose with meaningful experiences. You have helped others and shown great compassion to all beings. You are ready to make the journey."

As the Reaper gently took Giselle's soul, they vanished from the kitchen. Her lifeless body remained on the floor as the 911 operator's voice echoed through the room from the phone in Giselle's hand, urging her to hold on; help was on the way.

The Fractured Mind

THE MANSION ROSE HIGH on a hill, its spires piercing the sky like the crown of an ancient monarch. It stood proud yet weary, with ivy crawling along the stone walls, whispering stories of forgotten generations. A circular driveway wound through meticulously maintained and manicured gardens, which bloomed year-round under the care of the devoted groundskeeper. At the center of the driveway sat a grand marble fountain, its water cascading gracefully in the evening glow.

The estate's grounds stretched endlessly, bordered by dense woods on one side and sprawling meadows on the other. Sculpted hedges lined the walkways, and statues—weathered but dignified—peeked from beneath towering oak trees. A tennis court lay at one corner of the estate, and a pool at the opposite corner. Beyond the pool, a greenhouse housed exotic plants from across the globe, a relic of Vandyke's late mother's eccentric passions.

Inside, the house was no less impressive. The grand foyer welcomed visitors with polished marble floors that reflected the soft glow of crystal chandeliers. Long hallways stretched in every direction, leading to rooms adorned with oil paintings, intricate rugs, and heavy drapes. A library, filled with towering shelves of books, occupied an entire wing of the house. The dining room was fit for a king, with a table that could seat twenty, though it was always set for just five.

Vandyke arrived at the estate in the early evening. As his chauffeur unloaded luggage from the sleek black car, Vandyke's heart raced with both excitement and unease.

Four individuals stood waiting at the door: an athletic man with shaggy brown hair and a carefree stance, a sharp-dressed man with discerning eyes, and two twin sisters who stood side by side, mirroring each other's expressions of quiet amusement and subtle disdain.

The butler, standing discreetly to the side, opened the heavy oak doors to welcome Vandyke home. "Welcome back, sir," he said with a graceful bow, but his eyes betrayed a flicker of concern.

The staff had served Vandyke's family for generations, and they knew better than to question the peculiar dynamics within the house. The family had always carried with it a history of unspoken troubles, and the staff, bound by loyalty and tradition, simply went along with it—it was their duty to care for the family, no matter how strange things became.

Vandyke greeted each individual warmly. He always accepted them without hesitation, convinced that they were companions or relatives of his parents, though he could never quite recall how they came to live there.

Days turned into weeks, and the routines within the mansion settled into a rhythm. Meals were taken together at the grand dining table, the butler serving them with precise care. The sisters, often whispering conspiratorially, sipped tea in the parlor or strolled the grounds arm in arm. The sporty man came and went as he pleased, always late to meals and often drenched from the pool, much to the annoyance of the others. The sharp-dressed man, aloof and superior, spent hours in the library, rearranging books to suit his particular tastes.

As time passed, tension simmered beneath the surface. Suspicion and paranoia took root among the housemates. Vandyke found himself at odds with them all, his frustration mounting each day.

The sisters, bound by blood and a shared distrust of everyone, whispered their schemes in the privacy of their adjoining rooms. They had never liked the sporty man—his carefree nature, his disregard for schedules, the way he strutted about the estate as if it belonged to him. They didn't trust him, and in the quiet understanding that only twins could share, they decided he had to go. If they were to survive, he couldn't be allowed to stay.

The opportunity presented itself on a warm evening, when the air was thick with the scent of blooming jasmine. The sporty man, unaware of the malice brewing behind their identical smiles, announced his intention for an evening swim. He walked toward the pool, towel slung over his shoulder, utterly oblivious. The sisters watched from the balcony, exchanging a glance.

"Now," one of them whispered, her lips curling into a smile.

They slipped into silk bathing suits, their movements synchronized, as if they were preparing for an elegant soirée rather than a murder. They followed him to the pool, their faces calm, betraying none of the darkness hidden beneath their polished exteriors.

The sporty man grinned when they arrived, waving them into the water with boyish charm.

"Come on, the water's perfect," he called, floating lazily on his back, his arms spread wide.

The sisters waded in slowly, circling him like sharks around their prey, their delicate hands trailing the water's surface. The man laughed, splashing them playfully, unaware that his fate had already been sealed.

When the moment came, they struck without hesitation. One sister dove beneath the surface, wrapping her arms around his legs briefly to unbalance him. The other pressed her hands on his chest and shoulders, forcing him under. As the man thrashed, the sister below released her hold and surfaced, joining her sibling in restraining him. His grin twisted into panic as his arms flailed, feet kicking desperately against the water.

His struggles were fierce at first—churning waves slapping against the pool's edge, his head breaking the surface for brief, gasping moments. But the sisters held fast, their dainty fingers turned into merciless instruments of death. They whispered soothingly, as though calming a restless child, while the life drained from his eyes. Bubbles rose from his mouth, each one smaller than the last, until the water grew still.

He was gone. The ripples faded, and the pool returned to its serene, glassy surface, as if nothing had happened. The sisters lingered a moment, watching the moonlight glimmer on the water, satisfied with the silence. It was done.

The sisters moved with quiet efficiency, each performing her task without the need for words. With smooth, practiced motions, they guided the sporty man's lifeless body through the water and hauled him onto the pool's edge. Their eyes met briefly, a shared, unspoken understanding passing between them.

"No one will miss you," one of them whispered with a sly grin as they began the grim task of moving the body. The faint scent of chlorine clung to his clothes, making one sister wrinkle her nose.

"You always did leave a mess."

They worked in sync, dragging him across the ground, his limp body thudding softly against the earth as they headed toward the forest beyond the estate. The undergrowth rustled underfoot, the dark canopy above them concealing their movements. Neither spoke as they disappeared into the shadows, ensuring no trace of him would be left behind.

With the sporty man gone, Vandyke's unease deepened. The sisters were always huddled together, whispering in corners, their eyes flickering toward him with unsettling intent. He could feel their schemes brewing, convinced that if he didn't act first, they would turn their attention to him next. He felt sure somehow that they had played a role in the sporty man's disappearance and was certain he was now their next target.

One evening, as they gathered in the parlor, Vandyke offered them tea. The sisters sipped from their cups, unaware of the poison hidden within. It left no trace on their tongues, and as they continued their conversation, their voices slowly faded into silence. Their teacups slipped from their hands, shattering as they hit the floor. Moments later, they slumped in their chairs, lifeless.

Vandyke sat across from their still bodies, breathing heavily, his pulse pounding in his ears.

The room felt heavier, like the walls themselves bore witness to what had just unfolded. His hands trembled, not from fear, but from the overwhelming relief that he had saved himself from the betrayal that was inevitable. They couldn't hurt him now. But the bodies … the bodies were a problem. They couldn't stay.

Vandyke's mind buzzed with plans. They were everywhere, crowding his thoughts like scattered chess pieces waiting to be moved into place. He ran his fingers through his perfectly groomed hair, loosening it slightly, and paced the length of the room. There were no emotions in this task—just practicality. He had to get rid of them.

He glanced down at the lifeless forms slumped in their chairs, their expressions frozen in disbelief. A flicker of annoyance passed through him as he noticed the mess—the shattered teacups, the spilled tea soaking into the carpet, staining the fine upholstery. This wasn't how things were supposed to end. No matter. He would set it right.

He knelt beside the first body, the cold precision of his movements belying the storm raging beneath the surface of his mind. The first sister lay crumpled, her head at an unnatural angle. He rolled her body onto a heavy, embroidered rug. As the rich fabric enveloped her, he felt a grim sense of satisfaction. *They all thought they were clever,* he mused. *But I was always one step ahead.*

He dragged the rug toward the narrow servants' stairs at the back of the house, careful not to let the edges snag on the banister. His breathing was shallow but measured, and he paused only once to listen for movement. The house was silent, except for the faint ticking of a grandfather clock in the hall. He smiled to himself—*always on time.*

The stairs groaned beneath the weight, but Vandyke didn't falter. He'd practiced this in his mind many times before—how to move quietly, where to avoid making noise.

The cellar. The cellar was the answer. The house had been built long before his time, and its labyrinthine passages and storage rooms were perfect for his needs.

He made a second trip for the other sister—her body limp, poisoned, and still wrapped in her elegant shawl. Vandyke worked methodically, as if the task were nothing more than rearranging the furniture. He slid her lifeless form onto a thick wool blanket, careful not to disturb the graceful way the shawl fell over her shoulders. Wrapping her tightly, he bundled her like a parcel and hoisted her onto his back, staggering slightly under the weight.

The mansion was silent as he moved through the dim hallways, each step echoing softly against the hardwood floors.

He was efficient, quick, and deliberate. He placed the bodies in an old wine cellar, behind stacks of dusty bottles that hadn't been touched in years. He arranged them as neatly as one would store fine linens, aligning them with eerie precision, as if their placement mattered.

He went back upstairs to the room where they had drunk their last cup of tea and glanced around the room one last time, ensuring no trace of their presence lingered—no teacups left askew, no fallen hairpins to betray what had transpired.

There were moments when a flicker of doubt crept into his mind—moments when he wondered if he had gone too far. But no, this had to be done. *They were going to turn on me*, he reminded himself. *I didn't have a choice.*

Now, only Vandyke and the sharply-dressed man remained. Their interactions became tense, every glance loaded with suspicion.

"You can't trust me, Vandyke," the sharp-dressed man said one evening, swirling his glass of brandy. "And I can't trust you. One of us isn't leaving this house alive."

Vandyke's hand tightened around the knife in his pocket, the cool metal grounding him in the moment. "I know," he whispered.

The next day, their tension erupted into violence. They grappled on the third-floor balcony, each man desperate to gain the upper hand. The sharp-dressed man lunged first, shoving Vandyke toward the iron railing, the cold metal digging into his back. But Vandyke fought back, a desperate fury overtaking him. His hands clung to the man's coat as they struggled, and when the final moment came, they both went over the edge—locked together in a fatal dance.

They hit the ground with a bone-jarring thud, the impact sending a sharp pain through Vandyke's body. He gasped for breath, his limbs heavy and unresponsive. The life slowly ebbed from him, his broken body crumpled on the soft grass beneath the balcony.

The Grim Reaper materialized from the shadows like a ghost born of the night. His presence was not sudden but inevitable, as if he had always been there, waiting for the moment Vandyke's soul teetered on the edge. His dark cloak billowed gently despite the stillness in the air, swirling around him like smoke that knew no boundaries. The glint of his scythe caught the faint moonlight, a sliver of silver against the night. His hollow gaze rested on the broken man before him, as if seeing not only Vandyke's shattered body but the years of turmoil buried deep within his mind.

"It's over, Vandyke," the Reaper said softly, his voice devoid of judgment or malice, carrying only the weight of finality. "You don't have to fight anymore."

Vandyke blinked, his fading consciousness clouded with confusion. He tried to piece together the shattered fragments of his reality. "What ... what happened to them?"

The Reaper knelt beside him, placing a skeletal hand gently on his shoulder, the touch strangely comforting. "There were no others," the Reaper whispered. "It was always just you."

Vandyke's breath hitched as the truth unfurled before him, unraveling the carefully constructed illusions he had believed for so long. The housemates—his rivals, companions, and enemies—were nothing more than reflections of his fractured mind, figments conjured by a sickness that had consumed him. He had lived alone in the grand estate, ensnared in a relentless war with himself.

"You were sick, Vandyke," the Reaper whispered, the darkness in his voice tinged with unexpected tenderness. "None of this was your fault. Rest now. No one will harm you—not even yourself."

The weight of the Reaper's words settled over Vandyke, and for the first time in what felt like an eternity, the struggle ceased. There was no more need to fight, no more need to untangle the web of deceit and paranoia his mind had spun. *The battle was over, and peace beckoned at last.*

Vandyke lay still, the night closing in around him, his shattered body cradled by the soft grass beneath the balcony. And in that moment, he knew—*there was no one left to bury but himself.*

The staff, having heard the commotion and the fall, rushed to the garden. Some stood at the balcony, looking down in horror, while others gathered around Vandyke's broken body on the grass.

To them, it had always been Vandyke—no matter how differently he spoke or dressed, no matter how many people he seemed to be. They had known about his disorder but never questioned it, choosing instead to serve him with quiet loyalty, hoping to make his life easier in whatever small way they could.

They had observed him many times, going about his peculiar routines. On one occasion, they watched from the house as Vandyke splashed wildly in the pool, water flying in chaotic arcs as he moved around, mimicking the actions of someone grappling with another person. His movements were frantic, as if dragging an unseen weight across the water. Then, soaked to the bone, he climbed out of the pool and pretended to haul something heavy, straining as if dragging a lifeless body across the lawn. The staff exchanged uneasy glances but said nothing. They knew it was only Vandyke, playing out whatever scenario his mind had conjured.

Another day, they found him in one of the rooms, muttering to himself as he carefully rolled up rugs and gathered blankets. Teacups lay shattered on the floor, fragments scattered across the polished wood. He arranged everything meticulously, moving down the grand staircase with arms pretending to be full of something, carrying it to the cellar as if setting the stage for a hidden plot only he understood. The housekeeper had quietly swept up the pieces of the broken cups after he left, never once questioning him aloud. To do so would serve no purpose—Vandyke's reality was his own, and they had long learned to follow his lead without interfering.

Late that night, they had heard him on the balcony, his voice raised in a heated argument with no one. The wind carried fragments of his words, filled with frustration and anger, as though he were locked in battle with an invisible foe. His footsteps thundered across the floor, followed by a final, desperate scream from the balcony that echoed through the silent estate. The staff listened from the shadows, knowing better than to intrude. These outbursts were as much a part of their lives as polishing silver or lighting the fireplaces—they had long accepted that Vandyke's world was not one they could alter.

And now, as they gathered in the quiet of the night, they knew that the struggle was over. Vandyke was resting at last.

Paths to Redemption

Forgiveness opens the door to growth, healing, and a fresh start.

Signs

Ryan stood atop a fifty-story building, his heart pounding in his chest. His mind was a whirlwind of despair and regret. He had lost hope, convinced that he was beyond redemption. With tears in his eyes, Ryan took a deep breath and jumped.

His death was instant and brutal. As his body lay lifeless on the cold pavement, Ryan's soul began to drift away. In that moment, the Grim Reaper appeared, shaking his head in disappointment.

"Ryan, what have you done?" The Reaper's voice was a mixture of sorrow and understanding. "We weren't supposed to meet for another sixty-eight years, yet here we are." The Reaper paused, observing the shattered remains of Ryan's body. "I know this world has not been kind to you, but you did not have to go and jump off the top of a building. You've made a mess of yourself. Let's get going."

Ryan's soul hovered near his broken body, feeling the weight of the Reaper's words. He felt regret creeping in, mingled with a longing to return and undo what couldn't be undone. He could see the faces of those he loved and felt an overwhelming sadness. The Reaper continued speaking, his voice cutting through Ryan's despair.

"I understand why your hurt was so strong," the Reaper said, his voice a gentle admonition. "You had a heavy burden to bear. Sometimes life is unfair, and the mind can cloud reality. Humans have expectations—of each other and of life. When your life doesn't fit the mold, you panic and try to fix everything, not realizing that this is not how life works. Ryan, you know you shouldn't have taken your life. You didn't fulfill your purpose, and you've changed your destiny."

In his suspended state, Ryan realized the truth in the Reaper's words. He had let despair cloud his vision and allowed the actions of others to determine his worth.

The Reaper's tone softened. "I have something for you to do to change it again. There's a child walking the same path you did. He feels life is too hard, and he's building up the courage to end his pain. You must help him change course. Don't let him take the same path you did."

Ryan felt a stirring within him—a chance at redemption.

The Reaper paused, gauging Ryan's reaction. "This boy is destined for greatness. He's different for a reason. They make fun of him because they don't understand his mind is a wondrous thing. He's special, and his path is vital."

Ryan's soul quivered with a sense of purpose he had never felt before. Here was an opportunity to make a difference, to change a life that still held so much potential. The boy's path had been laid bare before him, a chance to guide, to protect.

The Reaper leaned closer, his voice a whisper of hope. "Help him focus his energy on his mind. Help him flourish and become the great inventor he's meant to be. I will give you the ability to communicate through signs. He's always asking the universe for these, so give him the guidance you wished for and never received."

Ryan nodded, understanding the gravity of his task. He had a second chance to make things right, to ensure this boy wouldn't face the same despair. The Reaper's gift of communication was a lifeline, not just for the boy but for Ryan himself.

With this new purpose, Ryan set to work. Over the years, he watched the boy grow, always ready to catch him when he fell. Whenever the boy asked for a sign, Ryan provided it, guiding him through the laughter and jeers of those who didn't understand him. The boy felt someone was watching over him, and he was not alone.

Ryan's presence was felt, not seen, but it was enough. Through subtle nudges and timely signs, he became the boy's unseen ally, a silent mentor who believed in his potential.

The boy grew into a remarkable inventor, known for his groundbreaking work in telepathic communication technology. He developed a device that allowed people to communicate with one another using only their thoughts, breaking down barriers and connecting individuals worldwide in a way never before imagined. His invention revolutionized the way humans interact, making communication faster and more intimate. Later in life, he became a respected professor, sharing his knowledge and inspiring countless others to pursue their dreams.

Ryan watched with pride as the boy—now a man—flourished. His guidance had helped shape a life that was destined to change the world.

When the inventor lay on his deathbed at the age of 98, surrounded by his loving family, the Grim Reaper appeared. The Reaper stood by the man's side as his soul began to depart from his body, the room filled with a serene peace. The Reaper was ready to guide him to the next chapter.

The man opened his eyes and smiled at the Reaper. He didn't fear death; he embraced it, knowing he had lived a fruitful life.

"Well done, Ryan," the Reaper said as he brought the man's soul to meet Ryan's. "Your work is complete. You've fulfilled your task beautifully."

Ryan and the man's souls met, a deep connection forming between them. The man didn't know why, but he felt a sense of familiarity and warmth with Ryan as if he had known him all his life.

The Reaper watched as the two souls walked by his side, guided by a bond that cut across time and space. Ryan had been there for the man throughout his life, without him knowing, and now, they were united in the afterlife.

A Light Returns

MARINA LAY ON THE cold, hard floor, her body broken and battered, the last remnants of light in the room dimming as her vision blurred. The only brightness came from a shattered lamp nearby, its bulb exposed, casting a harsh light that flickered weakly, almost like it was struggling to stay alive—just like her. She could feel the warmth of her own blood pooling beneath her cheek, seeping into the floor, mixing with the coldness of the tiles.

Above her, a shadow loomed. It was her husband, the man who had promised to love and cherish her but had done nothing but break her spirit and body. His face was a blur now, but his voice was clear, cutting through the darkness like a knife. "You're nothing, Marina," he sneered. "You're worthless. No one will ever want you. You're ugly, inside and out."

She remembered all the times he had said these things before, every time he had knocked her down, both physically and emotionally. His words had a way of burrowing into her soul, poisoning her thoughts, making her believe that she truly was worthless.

Marina had endured so much at his hands. She had been a good wife, or at least she had tried to be. She had wanted to create a loving home for their children, to raise them in a place filled with warmth and happiness. But all he ever did was tear her down, chip away at her self-worth until there was nothing left but a hollow shell of the woman she used to be.

She thought about all the times he had laid hands on her, each slap, punch, and kick a testament to the control he had over her. And every time, she had covered for him, too afraid to expose the truth, too desperate to believe that he might change. She had stayed silent, stayed by his side because he had made her believe that she had no other choice. That no one else would love her, that she was lucky to have him.

Deep down, Marina knew what she had always wanted—what every girl dreams of. She longed for a partner who would love her and take care of her, someone who would cherish her just as her father had hoped when he walked her down the aisle and placed her hand in her husband's. Every father wants his daughter to be treated with kindness, to be loved and cared for, to live a life filled with happiness and health, not to be abused, sad, and broken. As her father had watched her marry, he had believed that she was stepping into a life of joy, into the arms of a man who would protect her and make her feel safe. But that dream had turned into a nightmare, and the hands that were meant to comfort and protect had instead become the instruments of her torment.

Marina's father's voice echoed in her mind. He had always told her husband to take care of his baby girl, to cherish and protect her. Her grandmother, wise with age and experience, had seen through the facade. "Take care of her," she would plead. "Please, don't hurt her." And every time, he had promised to be a good man, to never harm her. He was a master of deception, fooling everyone around him, even her mother, who believed that he was a good man, worthy of her daughter's devotion.

Her mother's belief was born from her own painful experiences. She had endured the same torment in her youth, staying silent because, in her time, a woman didn't leave her husband. She stayed, even when it cost her happiness, because that was what was expected of her. It wasn't until her own husband nearly killed her that she found the strength to break free.

Everyone around Marina knew what was happening, but no one said a word. They saw the bruises, felt her tears, heard the whispers, but they kept silent because she was in love, and they didn't want to hurt her. They didn't know how to help her other than to be there to listen and plead for her to leave him. Marina felt alone in her suffering, trapped in a cycle of abuse that seemed never-ending.

As she lay on the floor, her strength slipping away, Marina thought about all of this. She wanted to be strong, to get up, to fight back, but she couldn't. Her body was too broken, her spirit too crushed. All she wanted was to be loved, to feel like she mattered, but all she had ever gotten was pain.

The darkness closed in around her, and she welcomed it, ready to be free from the torment. Before the last bit of light faded from her world, a figure appeared. At first, she thought it was just a trick of her mind, but then she realized it was real. The Grim Reaper stood beside her, his tall, cloaked form both terrifying and comforting. His face was hidden, but she could feel his presence, a strange mix of calm and power.

"Do you know why I'm here, Marina?" His voice was soft, almost tender, and it filled her mind as if he had spoken the words directly into her thoughts. She couldn't respond, her mouth unable to form the words, but he knew what she was thinking. She was sure he had come for her, that her time had finally come.

He knelt beside her, his hand resting gently on her forehead. "I am here for a soul, but not yours. First, there is something we must both do."

Marina's vision faded completely, the world going black as she slipped into unconsciousness. Even as she drifted away, she could still hear his voice, feel his presence. He told her that she was special, that she mattered, that she was beautiful and worthy of love. For the first time in years, she felt a warmth in her heart that had nothing to do with pain. The Reaper's words wrapped around her like a warm blanket, comforting her in the darkness.

When Marina awoke, the light had returned, and she heard a different voice—one that was filled with concern and love. "Mom, he's gone. You're going to be okay. He'll never hurt you or us again." It was her son, his voice breaking with emotion as he reassured her. The room was in chaos, destroyed by the violence that had taken place, but the most important thing was that the man who had tormented her was no longer a threat.

As the paramedics worked to lift her onto the stretcher, she glanced around the room. The police lights flickered outside, their red and blue hues blending with the flashing lights of the ambulance. And there, on the floor near the broken windows, was the lifeless body of her husband. He had opened fire on the police, and with a single shot to the head, they had killed him.

As they wheeled her out of the house, Marina's eyes locked onto the Grim Reaper standing over her husband's body.

He looked up at her. "It's not your time, Marina," he told her, as she was being wheeled away. "Your life can now begin. You are free now, free to find the love you deserve and to live the life you've always wanted."

Those words stayed with Marina as she recovered and as she started to rebuild her life. She found love everywhere—in her children, in her friends, in the simple joys of everyday life. She allowed her creativity to shape her identity, opening her heart to embrace the world and its new experiences. One day, she met a kind, gentle man in a bookstore, a place that had always been a sanctuary for her. He was different from anyone she had ever known.

Marina channeled her pain into her writing, sharing her story with the world and becoming a voice for those who had suffered in silence. Through her words, she offered hope and strength, reminding others that they were not alone and that happiness and love were still within reach. As she helped others heal, Marina found her own peace, rediscovering the strength and self-worth that had been buried for so long. In finding herself again, she not only reclaimed her life but also helped others reclaim theirs.

Ashes of Renewal

After the storm passes, the promise of new beginnings rises from the ashes.

The Forest

It was a beautiful, sunny day in the forest. The towering trees, their leaves rustling softly in the gentle breeze, cast dappled light across the forest floor. Birds chirped overhead, their songs filling the air, while squirrels darted between the trees, foraging for food. Humphrey, a young fawn with wide eyes and soft fur, ran and leapt quickly and energetically through the underbrush alongside his mother. She was his protector, his guide, always teaching him how to live in their lush, wild home. Today, everything seemed perfect—peaceful.

Humphrey paused, his little body still and focused as he caught sight of something unusual. A dark cloud loomed far away, thicker and darker than anything he had ever seen before. He wrinkled his nose. There was an unfamiliar smell, something sharp and unpleasant, curling through the air. His mother, who had been grazing nearby with the other deer mothers, lifted her head, her ears flicking in the direction of the cloud. She tried to hide her worry, but Humphrey could sense it.

The sky slowly darkened as the scent in the air grew stronger. Humphrey noticed the animals of the forest beginning to gather—rabbits, birds, foxes, bears, deer—everyone seemed to be moving in the same direction, away from the ominous cloud. At first, it was a steady pace, but as the cloud thickened and stretched across the sky, the movement turned into a brisk trot. The animals glanced over their shoulders, uneasy, feeling the heat that was now creeping in.

The brisk trot turned into a full sprint. The dark cloud was now a solid wall of smoke, and through it, flashes of red and orange flickered like monstrous claws. Flames. The forest, their home, was on fire.

Humphrey's heart pounded as he ran with his mother and the others, but he wasn't as fast as the older animals. His little legs struggled to keep up, and soon he and the younger animals fell behind. Their parents slowed to stay close, but the fire was moving too fast. The trees ignited, burning bright in the thickening air. Ash rained down, and the smoke choked their breath.

Humphrey's mother, her sides heaving with exhaustion, did everything she could to protect her son. She ran beside him, nudging him forward with urgency. "Stay close," she urged, but the fire was unrelenting. In moments, it had overtaken them. Flames roared as trees snapped and cracked under the heat. Some animals fell to exhaustion, others to the flames. They could not outrun the inferno.

The heat pressed in. Humphrey's mother huddled over him, shielding him from the worst of it, her body trembling with fear and exhaustion. But there was nothing more she could do.

And then, as the flames closed in, a figure appeared—dark and cloaked in a black robe, holding a scythe that shimmered against the backdrop of the fire. The Grim Reaper had come.

Humphrey's mother saw him first. Her eyes met the Reaper's, and she understood. This was the end. Her body sagged as the Reaper reached out, and in an instant, her soul was freed from her suffering. *"My Humphrey..."* she called, her voice lingering in the air.

The Reaper, without speaking, communicated to her that Humphrey was already with her. She turned, and there he was—no longer in his physical form but standing as a pure, innocent soul, gazing up at the Reaper with wide, unknowing eyes. Humphrey had seen the Reaper seconds after his mother had, and the Reaper had already taken him before the pain could touch him. The fire had claimed their bodies, but their souls were now beyond its reach.

The Reaper, though silent, was a calming presence. He held his scythe with a gentle grace, and with it, he moved through time. In the briefest moment, he had been with every animal in the forest. Each one had their own experience—some, like Humphrey, met the Reaper before the fire consumed them; others saw him in their final moments, a silent guide to the next stage of existence. With each soul, the Reaper had been there, collecting them in the same moment but in a different time, moving through fractals of moments.

Humphrey, still confused, looked at the Reaper. "Why?" he asked, his voice filled with sadness. "Why did this happen? Why are we here, and not with our friends?"

The Reaper, though he did not speak aloud, answered. *"Fires in the forests claim many lives. It is a part of the cycle of this world. But your journey is not over, Humphrey."* With a gentle sway of his scythe, the scene around them shifted.

Suddenly, Humphrey and his mother were no longer in the charred remains of the forest. They stood in a new place, a place of beauty and wonder. The forest here was untouched—tall trees stretched into the sky, vibrant with life. The air was fresh, filled with the scent of flowers and the songs of birds. It was just like their home before the fire.

And there, in the distance, were their friends—other animals from the forest, gathered together. Though the fire had taken their lives, it had not ended their journey. They were all here, in this peaceful place, their spirits free and unburdened. Humphrey's heart lifted as he realized that, though they had lost their home, they had gained something more—a new beginning, together.

The Fallen

THE EARTH WAS UNSETTLED, a planet in motion, always shifting between moments of quiet and chaos. The oceans swelled with their usual rhythm, the skies churned with the soft hum of the wind, and the land—whether bustling cityscapes or still forests—seemed to exist in a delicate balance.

But over the last decade, a change had come, subtle at first, until it grew into something no one could ignore. This was not a plague, nor an epidemic, nor a war, earthquake, flood, or asteroid—none of the catastrophic events that had ravaged the Earth and its inhabitants throughout history. But it was the end of an era.

Something ancient had stirred beneath the deepest part of the sea, far below the surface where the world of light ended, and the blackness of the ocean floor began. For millennia, it had lain dormant, hidden within the Earth's core, waiting for the moment it would reawaken. When the time came, this unseen force began to rise, slowly making its way up through the layers of rock and water, until it finally emerged. Quietly, it moved across the planet, first through the seas, then onto the land, and finally into the air itself. It spread without sound, without warning, claiming its victims in mere moments. No one saw it coming. No one could fight it. And within hours, entire communities were gone.

The bodies of the fallen didn't linger. Sometimes they disappeared in hours, sometimes in minutes. Their physical forms dissolved into the air, their particles scattering back into the world they had once lived in. There was no trace left behind—no graves, no ashes, no need for burials. The Earth reclaimed them, swiftly and silently, as if they had never been.

Only a fraction of humanity survived. The rest vanished as quickly as they had lived, and those who remained found themselves living in a world that was both eerily empty and achingly beautiful. The survivors didn't wander aimlessly or causing harm to each other or the world they knew and loved—they gathered, they organized, and they began to understand that their purpose was only to continue. But there was something different about this new world. The animals, untouched by the mysterious force, roamed freely. There were no more cages, no more chains. The surviving humans cared for them, sharing the land in harmony, respecting the delicate balance between life and nature. It was as though they had finally understood their place in the world.

The Grim Reaper had been present since the beginning of time. He had seen the asteroid that struck the Earth millions of years ago, wiping out the dinosaurs and much of the planet's life. He had witnessed the rise and fall of empires, the great ice ages, the floods, plagues, and epidemics that had devastated civilizations. War, famine, and natural calamities like earthquakes had shaped the course of history. He had watched as humans built their cities, only to see them crumble, and through it all, he had collected the souls of every being that had ever lived and died.

From his perch atop the mountain, the dark-robed figure surveyed the world below. Stretched out in every direction—rivers flowing clear and pure, forests dense with life, and animals roaming freely across the land. It was a sight he had seen many times before. But this extinction was different. It was quiet. There were no great catastrophes, no fires, no explosions. Just the sudden, silent loss of human life, and the Earth, untouched by destruction, flourishing as it hadn't in centuries.

Two million souls a day—that was the scale of his task. Every single one passed through his hands, and he guided them from this life to the next. Time was not a barrier for him. He moved through it as easily as he moved through the world, bending it, stretching it, creating pockets where he could collect countless souls in the blink of an eye. From the cities to the deserts, from the highest mountains to the deepest seas, he was everywhere at once, ushering each soul to the next level of existence.

As the souls passed into his care, many had questions. Why had this happened? What had caused their sudden deaths? But the Reaper didn't answer. He never explained the forces at play, never revealed the mysteries of life and death. He simply communicated, without words, that it was their time. That was all they needed to know. His task was not to answer their questions, but to guide them. And so, he did.

The Earth, in the absence of its fallen human population, began to change. The waters sparkled under the sun, clear and unpolluted. The forests, once stripped bare, had grown dense and vibrant, stretching across the land as far as the eye could see. Birds soared high in the sky, their songs echoing through the air, while wild horses ran free across the plains, their hooves pounding the earth with a power that had long been suppressed.

For the Reaper, there was beauty in this. He had always been present at the turning points of history, a witness to human arrogance and the inevitable consequences of their actions. But now, for the first time in millennia, he saw the Earth as it had been before mankind had claimed it as their own. The air was clean, the land was pure, and life—true, unrestrained life—thrived once more. It was not the violent, chaotic extinction of old. This was a quiet transition, one that left the Earth better than it had been.

The survivors would continue with their lives. They always had. But this time, the Reaper saw hope. They had seen what the world could be without their interference. They had lived alongside animals, not as conquerors, but as guardians. Perhaps this time, they would finally learn and do better. But the Reaper knew that wasn't for him to decide. His role was simple—to collect the souls of the fallen and guide them to the next stage of their journey. He had seen too much to dwell on the possibilities of what might be.

As the Reaper stood atop the mountain, looking out over the world, the setting sun cast a soft golden light across the land, and the rivers glinted like threads of silver, winding through the dense forests below. It was a world renewed, a world that had found its balance once more.

For a moment, the Reaper allowed himself to appreciate it. The beauty, the peace, the simplicity of life continuing without the weight of human interference. But he didn't linger. There were more souls to collect, more lives to guide from one existence to the next. And so, with a final glance at the world below, he turned and resumed his eternal work.

The Earth would go on, with or without humanity.

And so would he.

The end is never the end.

My Inspiration

Over the course of sharing these stories, I have been deeply moved by the responses from readers and listeners. Your words have not only inspired me to keep writing but have also shown me the unique ways these tales resonate with each of you. Thank you for your kindness, your reflections, and for being part of this journey.

Your Words

"*Chronicles of the Grim Reaper* is a collection of stories that allows us to re-imagine the Grim Reaper as a guide between life and death. I really enjoyed that there are stories based on different time periods throughout the book. I loved the different interactions between the Grim Reaper and characters in each story. It allowed me to have hope that our loved ones can watch over us, and that someday we will be reunited with them. Or that some can receive a second chance at life or a second chance at redemption. Someday we will all have a chance to meet the Grim Reaper, and I hope we will not be afraid like we have always been taught to be. If you have ever wondered about what happens between life and death. I highly recommend reading the *Chronicles of the Grim Reaper*."

—MARE C.

"I absolutely love Griz Calderon's *Chronicles of the Grim Reaper*. The storytelling was captivating, and the characters really felt real. It's clear a lot of heart went into this book. The stories are just long enough to keep my attention but leaving me wanting to read on to the next one. Highly recommend these stories to anyone looking for a great read!"

—COLLEEN J.

"Wow, just wow ... if you're wanting some quick titillating stories which give an alternate and provoking perspective on life and death, look no further. *Chronicles of the Grim Reaper* by Griz Calderon is an amazing collection of tales which absolutely do not disappoint! In a world of social media reels, this refreshing compilation allows you to enter a magical and interesting realm of distinct characters and their delicious life-to-death stories—in a sitting! I enjoyed experiencing their unique life transitions but, moreover, seeing it through Death's eyes itself. Totally unexpected! The Reaper truly comes to life in this series and gives a unique, refreshing perspective on love, life, loss, and everything in between. A great nightly read!"

—TERI H.

"*Chronicles of the Grim Reaper* presents a refreshing take on an iconic character. This collection of stories beautifully weaves themes of sacrifice, mercy, care, and gratitude. Calderon challenges the traditional view of the Grim Reaper as merely a harbinger of death, instead portraying him as a figure that offers solace and gentle relief as one approaches the end of life's journey. I found this reimagining profoundly moving, and I cherished every moment of the experience."

—RAFAEL RUIZ DE VELASCO

"These short stories challenge readers to view death not as an end, but as a transformative passage, leaving a lasting impression on how we perceive life's final chapter. As someone who is terrified of dying, *Chronicles of the Grim Reaper* provided a comforting shift in perspective. Calderon's thoughtful storytelling turned death from something to fear into a complex, transformative process. The stories of regret, redemption, and healing allowed me to rethink death as not just an end, but a part of life's journey, leaving me with a sense of peace and acceptance I hadn't expected."

—LIA R.

"Your stories resonate with me, and I think about them and the endless possibilities of what happens to us."

—CELESTE C.

"*Chronicles of the Grim Reaper* gives a comforting view of death. The Chronicles view death from a perspective rarely considered and in doing so, it connects the reader with a view of life. I enjoyed the short stories and would recommend this book to anyone who has dealt with the death of a loved one or has had an experience of their own."

—HEATHER A. YARIN

"Thank you! I love your stories. The Reaper is a wonderful character. I honestly feel it's sacrilege that more ears don't hear them, and I wish more people found your channel."

—FIONA CAHILL

"The stories about the Grim Reaper you share deeply move us with the humanity behind each encounter. Far from being dark, they illuminate the path toward profound and transformative life lessons. Each page is an invitation to grow and embrace our fragility with courage and wisdom. Thank you for allowing me to be part of this very special journey!"

—SANDRA ALDANA

"*Chronicles of the Grim Reaper* is deep, entertaining, and definitely a good read for anyone that has ever believed in the existence of the Grim Reaper. The stories tackle deep and spiritual elements about the meaning of life, the consequences of our choices, and the finality of our final moments. Griz's approach of words on driving your imagination from very specific time periods to some of the most amazing and heavenly views to the darkest corners of death row is extraordinary. She carefully plotted the past, present and future of her characters and somehow this would inevitably lead them to their encounter with the Reaper. Some of the characters left questions or unfinished business in a story so she delivered them back in another story to give us some insight. Griz's stories have changed my perspective. Maybe the Reaper isn't the EVIL figure that once appeared to be sitting on the couch in my dark hospital room. I was so afraid that I would pull the sheets over my head. I now believe he can bring us comfort and help us find inner peace as we take our last breath. I look forward to more of Griz's books of stories."

—CLAUDIA D.

"I loved the stories. It was different. Everyone associates the Grim Reaper as a dark, sad, cold person. I loved how you transformed him into a cool dude watching over everyone. I loved the themes of love and loss. It makes one think about their life and how we should cherish it. Well put together stories."

—BERYL K.

"I like the creativity and imagination of Griz's stories. They make me wonder who will be next? I once thought he was lurking in the darkness in my bedroom, and I was paralyzed in fear. After reading her stories, I am no longer afraid."

—SEBASTIAN I.

"I have really enjoyed Griz's Reaper stories at bedtime. I believe the Reaper can appear at any time to take us into the next world. He comforts us in our last moments."

—STELLA LUNA

"I absolutely love these stories! They are so captivating and some of them even make me tear up. I love listening to them while I'm driving or getting ready for bed. The audio version is just fantastic."

—ANA V.

"I really enjoy listening to these while going to sleep. The stories are very captivating and interesting. Love all the stories."

—LUCAS V.

"A timeless saying holds true here: "Don't judge a book by its cover." This book is the perfect example. There are no ghouls or goblins, just captivating stories that pull you in and keep you hooked. Whether you choose to listen or read, it's a must-have experience."

—AL

"I absolutely love *Chronicles of the Grim Reaper*. It gave me a whole new perspective on the Grim Reaper. I see him differently now—not just as someone who comes because of death, but as someone who shows up when you need him most. He gives you a chance, brings comfort, and is there to help guide you. That's what I love about it. I love it, love it, love it—and I'll definitely keep reading!

—TAMMY H.

"Light in the Darkness" - "I love the artwork with which you illustrate your stories, the malevolent glint in the eyes of Francine's Demon is perfect."

—FIONA CAHILL

"The Hunt" - "Love this one. Very moving. I usually can't read or watch anything that has animals in it as I'm just so sensitive to animal abuse, but this was beautifully written. A lovely tale to hear cuddled up in bed with my puppy this morning. Well done, Reaper!"

—FIONA CAHILL

"The Visit" - "For some reason and beyond my own comprehension, these stories bring me comfort. The stories are thoughtful, and your voice is soothing. Thank you."

—BAEBO762

Acknowledgments

CREATING *CHRONICLES OF THE Grim Reaper* has been an incredible journey, and I am deeply grateful to everyone who supported me along the way.

To my loving partner, James, thank you for making this possible.

To my family—my incredible parents, Israel and Frances, and my wonderful sisters, Mare, Claudia, Ana, Lily, and my nieces and nephews, Celeste, Alex, William, and Lucas, and my great niece and nephews, Stella, Sebastian and Ben —thank you for your constant encouragement and belief in me. Your love and support have been a source of strength and inspiration throughout this project.

To my friends, Teri H., Rafael R. de V., Samantha C., Johnny J., Lisa-Marie J., Colleen J., Ross J., Carmen E., Paul E., Semira R., Hamid R., Jordan B., Heather Y., Kati L., Bernhard W., Celius E., Delvin J., Amanda P., Amanda T., Sandra A., Rik O., Andrea R., Catalina A., Marvin M., Marvin B., Lia R., Beryl K., and Tammy H., who read the stories as I wrote them, offering thoughtful feedback and cheering me on, your enthusiasm kept me inspired to keep writing.

To my YouTube and social media followers, thank you for your kind words, encouragement, and engagement. Your support has meant more than you know. One of you mentioned being a little in love with the

Reaper—and you're not the only one. We all find him fascinating, and it's hard not to fall in love with his character. Writing these stories has inspired me to write even more, and I'm constantly thinking about how to make his character even more powerful and compelling.

A special thanks to my editor, Colm Farren, for bringing clarity and polish to these stories, and to George Long, who brought the spirit of this book to life with his stunning cover design.

This book is the result of so many hands and hearts, and I am truly thankful for each and every one of you.

Author's Note

THIS COLLECTION OF STORIES has been a deeply personal and meaningful journey for me. Writing *Chronicles of the Grim Reaper* allowed me to focus my mind on something positive, something that not only helped me but that I hope will help others—whether they are looking for healing, hope, or simply a comforting story. As I wrote these tales, they gave me hope: hope that the afterlife is even more beautiful than death, and a reminder that love surrounds us. We only need to open our eyes to see it.

The Grim Reaper brought life to these stories, a paradox I found fascinating. The characters in these tales face situations that mirror life itself—unpredictable, sometimes planned but rarely developing as expected. Through their experiences, I wanted to explore the connections between people, the ideas that connect us, and the ideas that flow through the stories.

My hope for you, the reader, is that these stories inspire you to appreciate life, to do good, and to cherish every day. Life is precious, and death is a part of its beauty. I hope these tales leave you with hope: hope that you will see your loved ones again, hope that good can arise from hardship, and hope that life, even beyond death, finds a way.

Thank you for reading these stories, for your engagement, and for your support. As an independent author, your feedback is invaluable. If you enjoyed this book, I would be so grateful if you would leave a review and share these stories with others. Your thoughts not only help me grow as a writer but also help others discover this book.

Finally, this is not the end of the Grim Reaper's tales. There are more stories to come, and I hope you'll join me for *Chronicles of the Grim Reaper: Volume II*. Until then, thank you for letting these stories become a part of your world.

Stay Connected

Thank you for reading *Chronicles of the Grim Reaper: Volume I*!
If you enjoyed this book, please consider leaving a review here:

https://chroniclesofthegrimreaper.com/reviews
Your feedback means the world to independent authors and helps others discover these stories.

Stay updated and connected:
Visit my website: https://chroniclesofthegrimreaper.com
Subscribe to my YouTube channel:
https://www.youtube.com/@ChroniclesoftheGrimReaper

Follow along for updates, new stories, and future releases. I'd love for you to share these tales with others and join me on this journey as more stories come to life.

About the Author

Griz Calderon

Griz Calderon, a Texas native, has always been passionate about storytelling and the arts. She enjoys creating short, meaningful tales that engage readers and encourage them to see life's challenges in a new way.

Griz's writing journey began as she prepared for a trip and she searched for the perfect book about the Grim Reaper. When she realized she couldn't find a book that suited her tastes, she decided to start writing her own collection of short stories about the Grim Reaper.

Outside of writing, Griz has a rich professional background in various industries, including technology, health, entertainment, and automotive. She is also deeply passionate about animal rescue, arts, photography, music, and giving back to her community.

Griz shares her life with her four rescue dogs and is a proud advocate for animals in need. Having experienced life's highs and lows—including being brought back to life after a near-death experience—she brings authenticity and heartfelt emotion to her stories.

Griz lives by the simple yet profound motto: "Love and be loved." It's a phrase etched on a leather bracelet she wears every day, serving as a constant reminder of the importance of kindness and connection.

Griz is currently working on *Chronicles of the Grim Reaper—Volume II* and a children's book of fables inspired by her love for Aesop's Fables and Dr. Seuss.

Readers can connect with Griz at https://chroniclesofthegrimreaper.com or through social media platforms like Facebook, Instagram, X, TikTok, LinkedIn, and YouTube (*Chronicles of the Grim Reaper*).